Rufus M

The Inner Life

in large print

Rufus M. Jones

The Inner Life

in large print

Reproduction of the original.

1st Edition 2023 | ISBN: 978-3-36837-648-2

Verlag (Publisher): Outlook Verlag GmbH, Zeilweg 44, 60439 Frankfurt, Deutschland
Vertretungsberechtigt (Authorized to represent): E. Roepke, Zeilweg 44, 60439 Frankfurt, Deutschland
Druck (Print): Books on Demand GmbH, In de Tarpen 42, 22848 Norderstedt, Deutschland

THE INNER LIFE

BY
RUFUS M. JONES, A.M., LITT.D.
1917

INTRODUCTION

There is no inner life that is not also an outer life. To withdraw from the stress and strain of practical action and from the complication of problems into the quiet cell of the inner life in order to build its domain undisturbed is the sure way to lose the inner life. The finest of all the mystical writers of the fourteenth century—the author of *Theologia Germanica*—knew this as fully as we of this psychologically trained generation know it. He intensely desired a rich inner life, but he saw that to be beautiful within he must live a radiant and effective life in the world of men and events. "I would fain be," he says, "to the eternal God what a man's hand is to a man"—*i.e.* he seeks, with all the eagerness of his glowing nature, to be an efficient instrument of God in the world. In the *practice* of the presence of God, the presence itself becomes more sure and indubitable. Religion does not consist of inward thrills and private enjoyment of God; it does not terminate in beatific vision. It is rather the joyous business of carrying the Life of God into the lives of men—of being to the eternal God what a man's hand is to a man.

There is no one exclusive "way" either to the supreme realities or to the loftiest experiences of life. The "way" which we individuals select and proclaim as the only highway of the soul back to its true home turns out to be a revelation of our own private selves fully as much as it is a revelation of a *via sacra* to the one goal of all human striving. Life is a very rich and complex affair and it forever floods over and inundates any feature which we pick out as essential or as pivotal to its consummation. God so completely overarches all that is and He is so genuinely the fulfillment of all which appears incomplete and potential that we cannot conceivably insist that there shall be only one way of approach from the multiplicity of the life which we know to the infinite Being whom we seek.

Most persons are strangely prone to use the "principle of parsimony." They appear to have a kind of fascination for the dilemma of *either-or* alternatives. "Faith" or "works" is one of these great historic alternatives. But this cleavage is too artificial for full-rounded reality. Each of these "halves" cries for its other, and there cannot be any great salvation until we rise from the poverty of either half to the richness of the united whole which includes both "ways."

So, too, we have had the alternative of "outer" or "inner" way forced upon us. We are told that the only efficacious way is the way of the cross, treated as an outer historical transaction; and we have, again, been told that there is no way except the inner way of direct experience and inner revelation. There are those who say, with one of George Chapman's characters:

"I'll build all inward—not a light shall ope

The common out-way.

I'll therefore live in dark; and all my light

Like ancient temples, let in at my top."

Over against the mystic who glories in the infinite depths of his own soul, the evangelical, with excessive humility, allows not even a spark of native grandeur to the soul and denies that the inner way leads to anything but will-o'-the-wisps. This is a very inept and unnecessary halving of what should be a whole. It spoils religious life, somewhat as the execution of Solomon's proposal would have spoiled for both mothers the living child that was to be divided. Twenty-five hundred years ago Heraclitus of Ephesus declared that there is "a way up and a way down and both are one." So, too, there is an outer way and an inner way and both are one. It takes both diverse aspects to express the rich and complete reality, which we mar and mangle when we dichotomize it and glorify our amputated half. There is a fine saying of a medieval mystic: "He who can see the inward in the outward is more spiritual than he who can only see the inward, in the inward."

This little book on the "Inner Life" does not assume to deal with the whole of the religious life. It recognizes that the outer in the long run is just as essential as the inner. This one inner aspect is selected for emphasis, without any intention of slighting the importance of the other side of the shining shield. Men to-day are so overwhelmingly occupied with objective tasks; they are so busy with the field of outer action, that it is a peculiarly opportune time to speak of the interior world where the issues of life are settled and the tissues of destiny are woven. There will certainly be some readers who will be glad to turn from accounts of trenches lost or won to spend a little time with the less noisy but no less mysterious battle line inside the soul, and from problems of foreign diplomacy to the drama of the inner life.

THE INNER LIFE

CHAPTER I
THE INNER WAY

I
THE MOMENTOUS CHOICE

Every scrap of writing that sheds any light on the life of Jesus, and every incident that gives the least detail about His movements or His teaching are precious to us. One can hardly conceive the joy and enthusiasm that would burst forth in all lands, if new fragments of papyrus or of parchment could be unearthed that would add in any measure to our knowledge of the way this Galilean life was lived "beneath the Syrian blue." But it may now probably be taken for granted that the material will never be forthcoming—and it surely is not now in hand—for an adequate biography of Him. The lives of Jesus that have been written in modern times have a certain value, as suggestive revelations of what the writers thought He ought to have been or ought to have done, but biographies, in the true sense of the word, they are not. The Evangelists performed for us an inestimable service, but they did not furnish us the sort of data necessary for a detailed biography, expressed in clock-time language.

Our "sources" are much more adequate when we turn our attention from external events to the inner way which His life reveals, though they still allow for free play of imagination and for much fluidity of subjective interpretation. It is possible, however, I believe, to look through the genuine words that are preserved and to see, with clairvoyant insight, the inner kingdom of the soul in that Person whose interior life was the richest of all those who have walked our earth. There are curious little playthings to be bought in Rome. If one looks through a pin-hole peep somewhere in one of these tiny toys, one sees to his surprise the whole mighty structure of St. Peter's Cathedral, standing out as large as it looks in reality. Perhaps we can find some pin-hole peeps in the gospels that in a similar way will let us see the marvelous inner world, the extraordinary spiritual life, of this Person whose outer biography so baffles us.

Our first single glimpse of His interior life must be got without the help of any actual word of His. It is given to us in the gospel accounts of His discovery of His mission. How long the consciousness of mission had been gestating we cannot tell. What books He read, if any, are never named.

What ripening influence the days of toil in the carpenter shop may have had, is unnoted. What dawned upon Him as He meditated in silence is not reported. What formative ideas may have come from the little groups of "the quiet ones in the land" can only be guessed at. We are merely told that He increased in wisdom as He advanced in stature, which is the only conceivable way that personality can be attained. Suddenly the moment of clear insight came and He *saw* what He was in the world for.

It was usual for the great prophets of His people to discover their mission in some such moment of clarified inward sight. Isaiah saw the Lord with His train filling the temple, felt his lips cleansed, and heard the call "who will go?" Ezekiel saw the indescribable living creature with the hands of a man under the wings of the Spirit and heard himself called to his feet for his commission. So here, there was a sudden invading consciousness from beyond. The world with its solid hills appears only the fragment, which it is, and the World of wider Reality floods in and reveals itself. The sky seems rent apart, the Spirit, as though once more brooding over a world in the making, covers Him from above, and gives inward birth to a conviction of uniqueness of Life and uniqueness of mission. He feels Himself in union with His Father.[1]

This experience of the invading Life, awakening a consciousness of unique personal mission, brought with it, as an unavoidable sequence, the stress and strain of a very real temptation. The inner world of self-consciousness has strange watershed "divides" that shape the currents of the life as the mountain ridges of the outer world do the rivers. No new nativity, no fresh awakening, can come to a soul without forcing the momentous issue of its further meaning, or without raising the urgent question, how shall the new insight, the fresh light, the increased power be wrought into life? The deepest issues turn, not upon the choice of "things," but upon the choice of the kind of self that is to be, and the most decisive dramas are those that are enacted in the inner world before the footlights of our private theater. The temptation is described by the Evangelists in such conventional language and in such popular and pictorial imagery that its immense inner reality is often missed by the reader. This oriental, pictorial way of presenting the drama of the soul catches the western mind in the toils of literalism. The picture is taken for the reality. What we have here in the temptation, when we go into the heart of the matter, is the momentous choice of the kind of Person that is to emerge. It is the immemorial battle between the higher and the lower self within. It was the line of least resistance to accept popular expectation, to go forth to realize the dream of the age. A person conscious of divine anointing, fired with passionate loyalty to the nation's hopes, gifted with extraordinary power of moving men to new issues would feel at once that he had only to put himself forth as the expected Messiah in order to carry the enthusiastic people with him. Let him but come with the spectacular powers of the Messiah that was eagerly looked for, the power to turn stones to bread, to leap from the pinnacle of the temple without injury, to break the Roman yoke and make Jerusalem once again the city of God's chosen people—and success was sure to follow. God's ancient covenant was an absolute pledge to the faithful that He would in His own time make bare His arm and deliver His people. As soon as the anointed one appeared all the forces of the unseen world would be at his command and his triumph would be assured.

The appeal of a career like that is no fictitious "temptation." It is of a piece with what besets us all. It is out of the very stuff of nature. At some such crossroad we have all stood—with the issue of our inner destiny in unstable equilibrium.

Over against it, another "way" is set, another kind of life is dimly outlined, another type of anointed one is seen to be possible, another kingdom, totally different from the one of popular expectation, is descried. <u>This kingdom of His spiritual vision cannot come by miracle or by power</u>; it can come only through complete adjustment of will to the will of the Father-God. This anointed one of His higher aspiration will be no temporal ruler, no political king, no spectacular wonder-worker. He will rule only by the conquering power of love and goodness. He will venture everything on sheer faith in the Father's love and on the appeal of uncalculating goodness of heart and will. This new kind of life that draws Him from the line of least resistance is a life of utter simplicity, which discounts what the world calls "goods," which draws upon an unseen environment for its resources and which expands inwardly, rather than outwardly, after the manner of the green bay tree. The new "way" that opens to His sight, and that beckons Him from all other ways of glory, is a way of suffering and sacrifice, a way of the cross. It offers itself not because self-giving is a better way than an easy, happy path, but because it is the *only way* by which love in a world like ours can reach its goal; it is the only way by which the kingdom of God can be formed in the lives of men like us.

He came forth from those momentous days of inner struggle with the issue settled, and with the first step taken in the way of the Kingdom.

II
MAKING A LIFE

Our present-day age has a kind of passion for the study of developing *processes*. We do not feel quite at home with any subject until we can work our way back to its origin or origins and then follow it in its unfoldings, explaining the higher and more complex stages in terms of the lower and more simple ones.

That method, however, cannot be successfully used to unlock the secret of the gospels. We do not find beginnings here; we cannot follow genetic processes; we are unable to discriminate higher and lower stages of insight. We must launch out at the very start in mid-sea. Whatever words of Christ one begins with indicate that He has already arrived at an absolute insight—I mean, that He has found a way of living that is no longer relatively good, but intrinsically and absolutely good.

It is an inveterate habit with men like us to estimate everything in terms of relative results. We are pragmatists by the very push of our immemorial instincts. Our first question, consciously or unconsciously, is apt to be, what effects will come, if I act so, or so? Will this course work well? Will it further some issue or some interest? And this deep-lying pragmatic tendency—this aim at results—

appears woven into the very fiber even of much of the religion of the world.

Sometimes the results sought are near, sometimes they are remote; sometimes they are sought for this world, sometimes they are sought for the next world; sometimes the pragmatic aim at results is crudely and coarsely selfish, sometimes it is refined, or altogether veiled, but religion has no doubt often enough been an impressive kind of double-entry bookkeeping, the piling up of credits or of merits which some day will bring the sure result that is sought.

Just that entire pragmatic attitude Christ has left forever behind. His inner way, His interior insight, passes on to a new level of life, to a totally different type of religious aspiration and to another method of valuation. For Him the beyond is always within. The only good thing is a life that is intrinsically good; the only blessedness worth talking about is a kind of blessedness which attaches by a law of inner necessity to the character of the life itself. It makes no difference what world one may eventually be in—if only it is still a world of spiritual issues—goodness, holiness, likeness to God, will still constitute blessedness as they do in this world.

When once this insight is reached, it affects all the pursuits and all the valuations of the soul. All "other things" at once become secondary, and "entering into life," "seeking life," "finding life," becomes the primary thing. "Making a life" overtops in importance even "making a living"—the life is more than meat, more than raiment, more than gaining the whole world. It is better to enter into life halt and maimed—with right hand cut off and eye plucked out—than bend all one's energies to preserve the body whole and yet to miss *life*. The way to life is strait, the entering gate is narrow. One cannot *enter* without facing the stern necessity of focusing the vision on the central purpose, without getting "a single eye," without letting go *many things* for the sake of *one thing*.

Sacrifice, surrender, negation, are inherently involved in any great onward-marching life. They go with any choice that can be made of a rich and intense life. It is impossible to find without losing, to get without giving, to live without dying. But sacrifice, surrender, negation, are never for their own sake; they are never ends in themselves. They are involved in life itself.

One great spiritual law comes to light and becomes operative, as soon as the interior insight is won, as soon as the inner way is found: The law that *the soul can have what it wants*. This law of the interior life, of the inner way, Christ affirms again and again in varying phrase. The inner attitude, the settled trend of desire, the persistent swing of the will, are the very things that make life. The person who cherishes hate in his soul forms a disposition of hatred and must live in the atmosphere which that spirit forms. The person who longs for deeds that are wrong, and allows desire to play with free scope is inwardly as though he did the deed. He is what he wants to be. And so, too, on the other hand, the rightly fashioned will is its own reward and has its own peculiar blessedness. The person who hungers and thirsts for goodness will get what he wants. He who seeks, with undivided aspiration, will always find. He who knocks with persistent desire for the gates of life to open will see them swing apart for him to go through to his goal. He who asks, with the ground swell of his whole inner being, for the things which minister to life and feed its deepest roots, will get what he asks for. The very pity of the Pharisee's way of life is that he has his reward—he gets what he is seeking. The glory of the other way is the glory of the imperfect—the glory of living toward the flying goal of likeness to the Father in heaven.

III
THE SPIRIT OF THE BEATITUDES

In putting the emphasis for the moment on the inner way of religion, we must be very careful not to encourage the heresy of treating religion as a withdrawal from the world, or as a retreat from the press and strain of the practical issues and problems of the social order. That is the road to spiritual disaster, not to spiritual power. Christ gives no encouragement to the view that the spiritual ideal—the Kingdom of God—can ever be achieved apart from the conquest of the whole of life or without the victory that overcomes the world. Religion can no more be cut apart from the intellectual currents, or from the moral undertakings, or from the social tasks of an age, than any other form of life can be isolated from its native environment. To desert this world, which presses close around us, for the sake of some remote world of our dreams, is to neglect our one chance to get a real religion.

But at the same time the only possible way to realize a kingdom of God in this world, or in any other world, is to begin by getting an inner spirit, the spirit of the Kingdom, formed within the lives of the few or many who are to be the "seed" of it. The "Beatitudes" furnish one of these extraordinary pin-hole peeps, of which I spoke in a former section, through which this whole inner world can be seen. Here, in a few lines, loaded with insight, the seed-spirit of the Kingdom comes full into sight. We are given no new code, no new set of rules, no legal system at all. It is the proclamation of a new spirit, a new way of living, a new type of person. To have a world of persons of this type, to have this spirit prevail, would mean the actual presence of the Kingdom of God, because this spirit would produce not only a new inner world, but a new outer world as well.

The first thing to note about the *blessedness* proclaimed in the beatitudes is that it is not a prize held out or promised as a final reward for a certain kind of conduct; it attaches by the inherent nature of things to a type of life, as light attaches to a luminous body, as motion attaches to a spinning top, as gravitation attaches to every particle of matter. To be this type of person is to be living the happy, blessed life, whatever the outward conditions may be. And the next thing to note is that this type of life carries in itself a principle of advance. One reason why it is a blessed type of life is that it cannot be arrested, it cannot be static. The beatitude lies not in attainment, not in the arrival at a goal, but in the *way*, in the spirit, in the search, in the march.

I suspect that the nature of "the happy life" of the beatitudes can be adequately grasped only when it is seen in contrast to that of the Pharisee who is obviously in the background as a foil to bring out the portrait of the new type. The pity of the Pharisee's aim was that it could be reached—he gets his reward. He has a definite limit in view—the keeping of a fixed law. Beyond this there are no worlds to conquer. Once the near finite goal is touched there is nothing to pursue. The immediate effect of this achievement is conceit and self-satisfaction. The trail of calculation and barter lies over all his righteousness. There is in his mind an equation between goodness and prosperity, between righteousness and success: "If thou hast made the most High thy habitation there shall no evil befall thee; neither shall any plague come nigh thy dwelling." The person who has loss or trouble or suffering must have been an overt or a secret sinner, as the question about the blind man indicates.

The goodness portrayed in the "beatitudes" is different from this by the width of the sky. Christ does not call the *righteous person* the happy man. He does not pronounce the attainment of righteousness blessed, because a "righteousness" that gets attained is always external and conventional; it is a kind that has definable, quantitative limits—"how many times must I forgive my brother?" "Who is my neighbor?" The beatitude attaches rather to hunger and thirst for goodness. The aspiration, and not the attainment, is singled out for blessing. In the popular estimate, happiness consists in getting desires satisfied. For Christ the real concern is to get new and greater desires—desires for infinite things. The reach must always exceed the grasp. The heart must forever be throbbing for an attainment that lies beyond any present consummation. It is the "glory of going on," the joy of discovering unwon territory beyond the margin of each, spiritual conquest.

Poverty of spirit—another beatitude-trait—is bound up with hunger for goodness as the convex side of a curve is bound up with the concave side. They are different aspects of the same attitude. The poor in spirit are by no means poor-spirited. They are persons who see so much to be, so much to do, such limitless reaches to life and goodness that they are profoundly conscious of their insufficiency and incompleteness. Self-satisfaction and pride of spiritual achievement are washed clean out of their nature. They are open-hearted, open-windowed to all truth, possessed of an abiding disposition to receive, impressed with a sense of inner need and of childlike dependence. Just that attitude is its own sure reward. By an unescapable spiritual gravitation the best things in the universe belong to open-hearted, open-windowed souls. Again, in the beatitude on the mourner, He reverses the Pharisaic and popular judgment. Losses and crosses, pains and burdens, heartaches and bereavements, empty chairs and darkened windows, are the antipodes of our desires and last of all things to be expected in the list of beatitudes. They were then, and still often are, counted as visitations of divine disapproval. Christ rejects the superficial way of measuring the success of a life by the smoothness of its road or by its freedom from trial, and He will not allow the false view to stand; namely, that success is the reward of piety, and trouble the return for lack of righteousness. There is no way to depth of life, to richness of spirit, by shun-pikes that go around hard experiences. The very discovery of the nearness of God, of the sustaining power of His love, of the sufficiency of His grace, has come to men in all ages through pain, and suffering and loss. We always go for comfort to those who have passed through deeps of life and we may well trust Christ when He tells us that it is not the lotus-eater but the sufferer who is in the way of blessing and is forming the spirit of the Kingdom.

Meekness and mercy and peace-making are high among the qualities that characterize the inner spirit of the kingdom. Patience, endurance, steadfastness, confidence in the eternal nature of things, determination to win by the slow method that is right rather than by the quick and strenuous method that is wrong are other ways of naming meekness. Mercy is tenderness of heart, ability to put oneself in another's place, confidence in the power of love and gentleness, the practice of forgiveness and the joyous bestowal of sympathy. Peace-making is the divine business of drawing men together into unity of spirit and purpose, teaching them to live the love-way, and forming in the very warp and woof of human society the spirit of altruism and loyalty to the higher interests of the group. These traits belong to the inmost nature of God and of course those who have them are blessed, and it is equally clear that the Kingdom is theirs. There is furthermore, in this happy way of life, a condition of heart to which the vision of God inherently attaches. He is no longer argued about and speculated upon. He is seen and felt. He becomes as sure as the sky above us or our own pulse beat within us. We spoil our vision with selfishness, we cloud it with prejudices, we blur it with impure aims. We cast our own shadow across our field of view and make a dark eclipse. It is not better spectacles we need. It is a pure, clean, sincere, loving, forgiving, passionately devoted heart. God who is love can be *seen*, can be found, only by a heart that intensely loves and that hates everything that hinders love.

IV
THE WAY OF CONTAGION

We have seen that religion cannot be sundered from the intellectual currents, or from the moral undertakings, or from the social tasks of the world. It cannot be *merely* inward. It can preserve its inward power only as it lives in actual correspondence with its whole environment and becomes also outward. But the primary thing for Christ, we saw, was the attainment of an inner spirit, the seed-spirit of the Kingdom, the spirit of the beatitudes—the attainment of a type of life to which blessedness inherently attaches.

The question at once arises, how shall this inner spirit be spread and propagated? How is religion of the inner type to grow and expand? There are two characteristic ways of propagating religious ideas, of carrying spiritual discoveries into the life of the world. One way is the way of *organization*; the other way is the way of *contagion*. The way of organization, which is as old as human history, is too familiar to need any description. Our age has almost unlimited faith in it. If we wish to carry a live idea into action, we *organize*. We select officials. We make "motions." We pass resolutions. We appoint committees or boards or commissions. We hold endless conferences. We issue propaganda material. We have street processions. We use placards and billboards. We found institutions, and devise machinery. We have collisions between "pros" and "antis" and stir up enthusiasm and passion for our "cause." The Christian Church is probably the most impressive instance of organization in the entire history of man's undertakings. It has become, in its historical development, almost infinitely complex, with organizations within organizations and suborganizations within suborganizations. It has employed every known expedient, even the sword, for the advancement of its "cause," it has created a perfect maze of institutions and it has originated a vast variety of educational methods for carrying forward its truth.

But great as has been the historical emphasis on organization, it nevertheless occupies a very slender place in the consciousness of Christ. There is no clear indication that He appointed any officials, or organized any society, or founded any institution. There are two "sayings" in Matthew which use the word "Church," but they almost certainly bear the mark and coloring of a later time, when the Church had already come into existence and had formed its practices and its traditions. And even though the great "saying" at Cæsarea Philippi were accepted as the actual words of Jesus, it is still quite possible to see in it the announcement of a spiritual fellowship, spreading by inspiration and contagion, rather than the founding of an official institution. It is, no doubt, fortunate on the whole that the Church was organized, and that the great *idea* found a visible body through which to express itself, though nobody can fail to see that the Church, while meaning to propagate the gospel, has always profoundly modified and transformed it, and that it has brought into play a great many tendencies foreign to the original gospel.

Christ's way of propagating the truth—the way that inherently fits the inner life and spirit of the gospel of the Kingdom—was the way of personal *contagion*. Instead of founding an institution, or organizing an official society, or forming a system, or creating external machinery, He counted almost wholly upon the spontaneous and dynamic influence of life upon life, of personality upon personality. He would produce a new world, a new social order, through the contagious and transmissive character of personal goodness. He practically ignored, or positively rejected, the method of *restraint*, and trusted absolutely to the conquering power of loyalty and consecration. It was His faith that, if you get into the world anywhere a *seed* of the Kingdom, a nucleus of persons who exhibit the blessed life, who are dedicated to expanding goodness, who rely implicitly on love and sympathy, who try in meek patience the slow method that is right, who still feel the clasping hands of love even when they go through pain and trial and loss, this seed-spirit will spread, this nucleus will enlarge and create a society. If the new spirit of passionate love, and of uncalculating goodness gets formed in one person, by a silent alchemy a group of persons will soon become permeated and charged with the same spirit, new conditions will be formed, and in time children will be born into a new social environment and will suck in new ideals with their mother's milk.

Persons of the blessed life, Christ says, are the saving *salt* of the earth. They carry their wholesome savor into everything they touch. They do not try to save themselves. They are ready like salt to dissolve and disappear, but, the more they give themselves away, the more antiseptic and preservative they become to the society in which they live. They keep the old world from spoiling and corrupting not by attack and restraint, not by excision and amputation, but by pouring the preservative savor of their lives of goodness into all the channels of the world. This preservative and saving influence on society depends, however, entirely on the continuance of the inner quality of life and it will be certain to cease if ever the salt lose its savor, *i.e.* if the *soul* of religion wanes or dies away and only the outer form of it remains.

But such lives are more than antiseptic and preservative; they are kindling and illuminative. They become "candles of the Lord." Candles emit their light and kindle other candles by burning themselves up and transmitting their flame. When a life is set on fire, and is radiant with self-consuming love, it will invariably set other lives on fire. Such a person may teach many valuable ideas, he may organize many movements, he may attack many evil customs, but the best thing he will ever do will be to fuse and kindle other souls with the fire of his passion. His own burning, shining life is always his supreme service.

"The greatest legacy the hero leaves his race

Is—to have been a hero."

Such a person will be eager to decrease that his kindling power may increase. He will not care to save himself, or to reap a reward for his service. He may not even know that he is shining, like the early saint who "wist not that his face did shine." But for all that, men will see the way by his light and will catch the glory of living because he exhibits it. He can no more be hid than can a hill-top city, or the headlight of a locomotive, or the newly risen sun.

That is Christ's way of spreading the life of the Kingdom, that is His method of propagating the inner spirit, and of producing a society of blessed people.

V
THE SECOND MILE

It may seem to some incongruous to be writing about an inner way of life in these days when *action* is felt by so many to be the only reality and when in every direction outside there is dire human need to be met.

"Leave, then, your wonted prattle,

The oaten reed forbear;

For I hear a sound of battle,

And trumpets rend the air."

But more than ever is it necessary for us to center down to eternal principles of life and action, to attain and maintain the right inner spirit, and to *see* what in its faith and essence Christianity really means. Precisely now when the Sermon on the Mount seems least to be the program of action and the map of life, is it a suitable time for us to endeavor to discover what Christ's way means, by looking through the literal phrases in clairvoyant fashion to the spirit treasured and embalmed within the wonderful words?

There is one phrase which seems to me to be, in a rare and peculiar degree, the key to the entire gospel—I mean the invitation to go "the second mile": "If any man compel you to go a mile, go two miles." It is always dangerous, I know, to fly away from the literal significance of words and to indulge in far-fetched "spiritual" interpretations. But it is even more dangerous, perhaps, to read words of oriental imagery and paradox as though they were the plain prose speech of the occidental mind, and to be taken only at their face value.

There will probably always be Tolstoys—great or small—who will make the difficult, and never very successful, experiment of taking this and the other "commands" of the Sermon on the Mount in a literal and legalistic sense, but to do so is almost certainly to be "slow of heart," and to miss Christ's meaning. Whatever else may be true or false in our interpretations of the teachings of Christ, it may always be taken for certain that He did not inaugurate a religion of the legalistic type, consisting of commands and exact directions, to be literally followed and obeyed as a way to secure merit and reward. To go "the second mile," then, is an attitude and character of spirit rather than a mere rule and formula for the legs.

Christ always shows a very slender appreciation of any act of religion or of ethics which does not reach beyond the stage of *compulsion*. What is done because it *must* be done; because the law requires it, or because society expects it, or because convention prescribes it, or because the doer of it is afraid of consequences if he omits it, may, of course, be rightly done and meritoriously done, but an act on that level is not yet quite in the region where for Christ the highest moral and religious acts have their spring. The typical Pharisee was an appalling instance of the inadequacy of "the first-mile" kind of religion and ethics. He plodded his hard mile, and "did all the things required" of him. In the region of commands, or "touching the law" he was "blameless." But there was no spontaneity in his religion, no free initiative, no enthusiastic passion, no joyous abandon, no gratuitous and uncalculating acts. He did things enough, but he did them because he *had* to do them, not because some mighty love possessed him and flooded him and inspired him to go not only the expected mile, but to go on without any calculation out beyond milestones altogether. Just here appears the new inner way of Christ's religion. The legalist, like the rich young man, "does all the things that are commanded in the law," but still painfully "lacks" something. To get into Christ's way, to "follow" in any real sense, he must cut his cables and swing out from the moorings where he is *tied*. He must catch such a passion of love that giving either of his money or of himself, shall no longer be for him an imposed duty but rather a joy of spirit.

The parable of the "great surprise" is another illustration, a glorious illustration, of the spirit of the "second mile." The "blessed ones" in the picture (which is an unveiling of actual everyday life in its eternal meaning rather than a portraiture of the day of judgment) find themselves at home with God, drawn into His presence, crowned with His approval, and sealed with His fellowship. They are surprised. They had not been adding up their merits or calculating their chances of winning heaven. They are beautifully artless and naïve: "When saw we Thee hungry and fed Thee?" They have been doing deeds of love, saying kind words, relieving human need, banishing human loneliness, making life easier and more joyous, because they had caught a spirit of love and tenderness, and, therefore, "could not do otherwise," and now they suddenly discover that those whom they helped and rescued and served were bound up in one inseparable life with God himself, so that what was done to them was done to Him, and they find that *their* spontaneous and uncalculating love was one in essence and substance with the love of God and that they are eternally at home with Him.

The tender, immortal stories of the woman who broke her alabaster vase of precious nard and "filled all the house with the odor," and of the woman (perhaps the same one) who had been a sinner and who from her passion of love for her great forgiveness wet Christ's feet with her tears, even before she could open her cruse of ointment, are the finest possible illustrations of the spirit of "the second mile." They picture, in subtly suggestive imagery, the immense contrast between the spontaneous, uncalculating act of one who "loves much" and does with grace what love prompts; and acts, on the other hand, like that of Simon the pharisaic host, who offers Jesus a purely conventional and grudging hospitality, or like that of the disciples who sit indeed at the table with Jesus but come to it absorbed with the burning question, "who among us is to be first and greatest," not only at the table but "in the Kingdom!"

What grace and unexpected love come into action in the simple deed of the "Samaritan" who, from nobility of nature, does what official Priest and Levite leave undone! The hated foreigner, spit at and stoned as he walked the roads of Judea, under no obligation to be kind or serviceable, is the real "neighbor," the bearer of balm and healing, the dispenser of love and sympathy. He may have no ordination to the priesthood, but he finely exhibits the attitude of grace which belongs in the religion of "the second mile."

But we do not reach the full significance of "the second mile" until we see that it is something more than the highest level of human grace. What shines through the gospels everywhere, like a new-risen sun, is the revelation that *this*—this grace of the second mile—is the supreme trait and character-nature of God as well. How surprising and unexpected is that extraordinary unveiling of the divine nature in the story of the prodigal boy! It is wonderful enough that one who has wasted his substance and squandered his own very life should still be able in his squalor and misery to come to himself and want to go home;

but the fact which radiates this sublime story like a glory is the uncalculating, ungrudging, unlimited love of the Father, which remains unchanged by the boy's blunder, which has never failed in the period of his absence, and which bursts out in the cry of joy: "This my son was dead and is alive again, he was lost and is found."

It is, and always has been, the very center of our Christian faith that the real nature and character of God come full into view in Christ, that God is in mind and heart and will revealed in the Person whom we call Christ. "The grace," then, "of the Lord Jesus Christ," of which we are reminded in that great word of apostolic benediction, is a true manifestation of the deepest nature and character of God Himself. The Cross is not an artificial scheme. The Cross is the eternal grace, the spontaneous, uncalculating love of God made visible and vocal in our temporal world. It is the apotheosis of the spirit of the second mile.

CHAPTER II
THE KINGDOM WITHIN THE SOUL

I
BAGS THAT WAX NOT OLD

The ancient world found it very difficult to keep money even after it was got. There were almost constant wars involving the dire stripping of the unprotected country districts, and the siege and devastation of cities. In those times almost everything was fragile. It was never easy to discover any form of wealth that was surely abiding. Even if the besom of an invading army did not sweep away the labor of years, still there were other enemies to be feared. Tyrants were, always on the watch for ways of relieving wealthy men of their treasures. There were robber bands lying in wait for the traveler, and neighborhood thieves found it a small matter to break into private houses and to steal hidden money. It was no uncommon thing for men to dig in the ground and hide the talent which they had saved, or to bury the pearl of great price, or other precious jewel, in a field. If one invested his wealth in garments, then another enemy was to be feared. The moth is as old as clothes, and he got in even where the thief failed to break through.

The problem of getting an indestructible money-bag was, thus, a problem of first importance. A journey to Jericho might any day reduce a man to primitive conditions, or a passing army might make him a beggar, or the visit of a thief might strip him of all his living, or the silent work of a brood of moths might ruin the savings of years. There were no perdurable purses, no nonbreakable banks, no irreducible forms of wealth.

Christ evidently recognized that there was a value in money. He did not apparently demand from his follower the absolute renunciation of ownership. He expounded no new theory of economics. But he was profoundly impressed by the moral havoc and the social calamities caused by the excessive ambition for, and pursuit of, wealth. He saw how the mad rush for money and the overvaluation of it killed out the noblest fundamental traits of the soul, and, more than all else, he felt the tragedy of human lives being focused with intensity of strain and fixed with burning passion on the pursuit of such pitiably fragile treasures—money-bags of all sorts waxing old and becoming incapable of holding the hoard that absorbed the whole life.

Christ, then, proposes a new kind of purse, an indestructible and immutable treasure-bag—"make for yourselves bags that wax not old." Such purses are not on the market, they cannot be purchased, they must be woven by each person for himself, and they must be woven, if at all, out of the stuff of *life* itself. We here pass over, as so often in Christ's teaching, from extrinsic wealth to intrinsic, from the wealth which men merely possess to the kind of wealth which they can themselves *be*. We once more find ourselves brought to an inner way of living, where the issue is no longer how to accumulate goods, but rather how to become good. The problem is the problem of what men live by. We are called to loosen our grip on perishable treasures only that we may tighten our hold on heavenly, *i.e.* spiritual, treasure. We are shown the folly of spending a life building barns for expanding earthly possessions, while we are taking no pains to make ourselves rich in God.

What is it, then, that men live by? What will prove to be imperishable wealth, whether we are in this world, or in any other world of real moral issues? It is obviously not money, for men often live nobly after the money-bag has waxed old and after the bank has failed, and it is our most elemental faith that life blossoms out into its consummate richness after all earthly affairs come to a complete close, and after every penny of visible wealth has been left forever behind. Money is plainly not intrinsic treasure; love is, goodness is, joy is. A beloved disciple, in a moment of inspiration, announced the profound truth that love is "of God." Men wrongly divide love into two types, "human love" and "divine love," but in reality there is only *love*. Wherever love has become the nature of the soul, and it has become "natural" now to forget self for others, to seek to give rather than to get, to share rather than to possess, to be impoverished in order that some loved one may abound, there a divine and Godlike spirit has been formed. And we now come upon a new kind of wealth, a kind that accumulates with use, because it is a law that the more the spirit of love is exercised, the more the soul spends itself in love, so much the more love it has, the richer it grows, the diviner its nature becomes. But at the same time, it is a fact that love is never complete, never reaches its full scope and measure until our love takes on an eternal aspect—until we love God in Himself or love Him in our loved ones. One reason why love is exalted by death is that we no longer love our immortal loved one in any narrow and selfish way; we love now for pure love's sake, and the truest of all treasures which can be laid up in imperishable bags is this stock of unalloyed love for that which is most lovely—for God and for souls that are given to us to bring some of His nature closer to our human hearts.

Goodness is, of course, notoriously hard to define. It is never an abstract quality that can be described by logical concepts. It is a way of living, a way of acting, a way of working out relationships. It is, like love, a cumulative thing. To be good inherently means to be becoming better, to be on the way to an unattained goal of action, or of character. It is the glory of going on to be perfect like our Father in heaven. To be rich in goodness of character, therefore, is to be on the way to become ever richer, however long the journey lasts, however far the spiral winds, for goodness, like love, is of God, and steadily assimilates our imperfect human nature to the perfect divine nature.

Joy is, perhaps, not often thought of as one of the things men live by, as the soul's eternal wealth. Life is so full of sorrow and pain that joy seems like a fleeting, vanishing asset. But that is because joy is confused with pleasure. True joy is not a thing of moods, not a capricious emotion, tied to fluctuating experiences. It is a state and condition of the soul. It survives through pain and sorrow and, like a subterranean spring, waters the whole life. It is intimately allied and bound up with love and goodness, and so is deeply rooted in the life of God. Joy is the most perfect and complete mark and sign of immortal wealth, because it indicates that the soul is living by love and by goodness, and is very rich in God.

II
OTHERISM

(Matt. VII. 1-12)

Altruism is an honored word. Otherism is only recently coined and has not yet become widely current in good speech. We need, however, a word that has more inward depth than altruism usually carries, and perhaps otherism will eventually take that vacant place.

Not merely in these days of war, but in all our human relations all the time we greatly need to get the interior vision which enables us to understand from within those with whom we live and work. Nobody sees life correctly until he has corrected his own views by a true appreciation of the views of others. From the outside it is impossible to estimate any life fairly. We have long ago learned that we can get no true account of any historical character unless we have a historian who can put himself in the place of the person he is describing. He must have imagination and be able to see clearly the conditions and forces, the influences and the atmosphere in which the man lived. The problems which he had to deal with, the conceptions which governed men's thoughts when he lived—all these must be understood, before we can get any estimate of the man himself. The same sort of imagination is necessary to judge the person who lives next door. We dare not pronounce upon him until we know all that he has to face. If we could once feel his quivering spirit and could see his inward struggles, we could not set up our private tribunal and pass our cold individual judgment upon him. The real remedy for this hard critical spirit which breaks society up into independent units is the spirit of love, the spirit of otherism.

The moment we put ourselves in the place of others, and pronounce no judgment upon persons until we have seen all the circumstances of their life, a new state of things at once appears. Genuine sympathy, clear interior insight into the personality of others, immediately creates a new world. The trouble too often is that we see all the defects in others and forget our own. We want to take the mote out of another person's eye while all the time there is a whole fence rail in our own. Christ's rule is to make oneself perfect before one goes to correcting others. "Let him who is without sin cast the first stone."

There is another situation also which would be remedied if we learned to put ourselves in the other person's place—if we had the spirit of otherism. Christ sums it up in the proverb about *casting pearls before swine, i.e.* giving what is a misfit. Many of our well-meant charities are of this sort. We blunder in our efforts to help poor needy people, because we do not get their point of view. We do not live our way into their lives. There is no fit between our gift and their need. They get a stone for bread.

The same thing happens in much of our public speaking. Many persons have the barbarous habit of never imagining the listeners' point of view. They go on speaking as unconscious of the condition confronting them as the hose pipe is when the water is turned on. The remedy again is otherism. It is impossible to help anybody with a message until you can in some measure *share* his life.

"The Holy Supper is kept, indeed,

In whatso we share with another's need."

This teaching is all summed up in the golden rule, "All things that ye would that men should do unto you do ye also unto them." It is clear at once that to do this one must cultivate both his spirit of love and his power of imagination. It is never enough to want to help a person. We must put ourself in his place and be able to do what really *will help him*. It would appear, therefore, that the most difficult and at the same time the most heavenly attainment in the world is sympathy—the spirit of otherism.

III
SCAVENGERS AND THE KINGDOM

We no longer expect a world of perfect conditions to appear by sudden intervention. We have explained so many things by the discovery of antecedent developmental processes that we have leaped to the working faith that all things come that way. We do, no doubt, find unbridged gaps in the enormous series of events that have culminated in our present world, and we must admit that nature seems sometimes to desert her usual placid way of process for what looks like a steeplechase of sudden "jumps," but we feel pretty sure that even these "jumps" have been slowly prepared for and are themselves part of the process-method.

Then, too, we find it very difficult to conceive how a spiritual kingdom—a world which is built and held together by the inner gravitation of love—could come by a fiat, or a stroke, or a jet. The qualities which form and characterize the kingdom of God are all qualities that are born and cultivated within by personal choices, by the formation of rightly-fashioned wills, by the growth of love and sympathy in the heart, by the creation of pure and elevated desires. Those traits must be won and achieved. They cannot be shot into souls from without. If, therefore, we are to expect the crowning age that shall usher in a world in which wrath and hate no longer destroy, from which injustice is banished and the central law of which is love like that of Christ's, then we must look for this age, it seems to me, to come by slow increments and gains of advancing personal and social goodness, and by divine and human processes already at work in some degree in the lives of men.

Christ often seems to teach this view. There is a strand in his sayings that certainly implies a kingdom coming by a long process of slow spiritual gains. There is first the seed, then the blade, then the ear and finally the full corn in the ear. The mustard seed, though so minute and tiny, is a type of the kingdom because it contains the potentiality of a vast growth and expansion. The yeast is likewise a figure of ever-growing, permeating, penetrating living force which in time leavens the whole mass. The kingdom is frequently described as an inner life, a victorious spirit. It "comes" when God's will is done in a person as it is done in heaven, and, therefore, it is not a spectacle to be "observed," like the passing of Cæsar's legions, or the installation of a new ruler. But, on the other hand, there are plainly many sayings which point toward the expectation of a mighty sudden *event*. We seem, again and again, to be hearing not of process, but of apocalypse, not of slow development, but of a mysterious leap. There can be no question that most devout Jews of the first century expected the world's relief expedition to come by miracle, and it is evident that there was an intense hope in the minds of men that, in one way or another, God would intervene and put things right. Many think that Christ shared that hope and expectation. It is of course possible that in sharing, as He did, the actual life of man, He partook of the hopes and travails and expectations of His times. But, I think, we need to go very slowly and cautiously in this direction. To interpret Christ's message mainly in terms of apocalypse and sudden interventions is surely to miss its naturalness, its spiritual vision, and its inward depth. We can well admit that nobody then had quite our modern conception of process or our present day dislike of breaks, interruptions, and interventions. There was no difficulty in thinking of a new age or dispensation miraculously inaugurated. Only it looks as though Christ had discovered an ethical and spiritual way which made it unnecessary to count on miracle. There was much refuse to be consumed, much corruption to be removed, before the new condition of life could be in full play, but He seems to have seen that the consuming fire and the cleansing work were an essential and inherent part of the *process* that was bringing the kingdom.

When he was asked *where* men were to look for the kingdom, His answer was that they were to find a figure and parable of it in the normal process of nature's scavengers. The carcass lies decaying in the sun, corrupting the air and tainting everything in its region. There can be no wholesome conditions of life in that spot until the corruption is removed. But nature has provided a way of cleansing the air. The scavenger comes and removes the refuse and corruption and turns it by a strange alchemy into living matter. Life feeds on the decaying refuse, raises it back into life, and cleanses the world by making even corruption minister to its own life processes. We could not live an hour in our world if it were not alive with a myriad variety of scavenging methods that burn up effete matter, transmute noxious forms into wholesome stuff, cleanse away the poisons, and transmute, not by an apocalypse, but by a process, death into life and corruption into sweetness. May not the vulture, like the tiny sparrow who cannot fall without divine regard, be a sign, a figure, a parable? When we look for the kingdom, in the light of this sign, we shall not search the clouds of heaven, we shall not consult "the number of the beast"—we shall look for it wherever we see life conquering death, wherever the white tents of love are pitched against the black tents of hate, wherever the living forces of goodness are battering down the strongholds of evil, wherever the sinner is being changed to a saint, wherever ancient survivals of instinct and custom are yielding to the sway of growing vision and insight and ideal. It is "slow and late" to come, this kingdom! So was life slow to come, while all that was to be

"Whirl'd for a million æons thro' the vast

Waste dawn of multitudinous-eddying light."

So was man slow to come, while fantastic creatures were "tearing each other in the slime." So was a spirit-governed Person slow to come, while men lived in lust and war and hate. But in God's world at length the things that ought to come do come, and we may faintly guess by what we see that the kingdom, too, is coming. There is something like it now in some lives.

IV
"THE BEYOND IS WITHIN"

Among the parables of Christ there is a very impressive one on the shut door. It is a story of ten country maidens who were invited to a wedding. They were to meet the bridegroom coming from a distance, as soon as his arrival should be announced, and with their lighted lamps they were to guide him and his attendants through the darkness to the home of the bride, where the banquet and the festal dance were to be held.

For many days these simple maidens had been living in the thrilling expectation of the great event in which they were to take a leading part.

They had been busy with their preparations, drilling their rhythmic steps, and talking eagerly of the approaching night. But five of them foolishly neglected the critically important part of the preparation—they took no oil to supply their lamps and at the dramatic moment they found themselves compelled to withdraw from the joyous throng and to go in search of the necessary equipment. When at length they arrived with their oil, the illuminated procession was over and the door of the festal house was shut.

The simple maidens soon discovered that there was a stern finality to this shut door. Their blunder had irrevocable consequences. They may have had other interesting opportunities as life went on, but they forever missed this joyous procession and this wedding feast. "Too late, too late. Ye cannot enter now."

Christ turns this common, trivial neighborhood incident into a parable of the Kingdom of God. Those who believe that He was looking, as so many in His time were looking, for a sudden shift of dispensations and for a Kingdom to be ushered in by a stupendous apocalyptic event, find in this irrevocably shut door of the parable a figure of the doom of those who failed to prepare for the sudden coming of this crisis, decisive of the destiny of men.

But there is another, and, I think, a truer, way of interpreting this shut door. There is a stern finality to all opportunities that have been missed and to all high occasions that have been blundered and bungled. All decisions of the will, all choices of life have, in their very nature, apocalyptic finality. They suddenly reveal and unveil character and they are loaded with destiny which can be changed only by a change of character. Other opportunities may offer themselves and new chances may indeed come, but when any choice has been made or any opportunity has been missed that chance has gone by and that door is shut.

The football player who has had a chance in the great game of the year to make a goal, and instead of doing it fumbled the ball and lost the opportunity to score, may just possibly have another chance sometime, but no apologies and no explanations can ever change the apocalyptic finality of that fumble.

Something like that is involved in all the spiritual issues of life, and our deeds and attitudes are all the time irrevocably opening or shutting doors, which prove to be doors to the Kingdom of God. Christ may possibly at times have looked for some sudden revelation of destiny, but surely for the most part He looked for the momentous issues of the Kingdom *within the soul itself* rather than in a spectacular event in the outer world. This principle throws light on all Christ's sayings about the future. The coming destiny is not in the stars, it is not in the sentence of a Great Assize, it is not in the sudden shift of "dispensations"; it is in the character and inner nature, as they have been formed within each soul. The thing to be concerned about is not so much a day of judgment or an apocalyptic moment, as the trend of the will, the attitude of the spirit, the formation of inner disposition and character. We are always facing issues of an eternal aspect, and every day is a day of judgment, revealing the line of march and the issues of destiny. Conversion crises are fortunately possible, when suddenly a new level of life may be reached and a fresh start may be made, and in this inner world of personality, there are always new possibilities occurring, but, as at oriental marriage feasts, neglected opportunities are irreversibly neglected, shut doors are irrevocably shut, and blunders that affect the issues of the soul have an apocalyptic finality about them. New dispensations may await us; the Kingdom may come in ways we never dreamed of; the beyond may be more momentous than we have ever expected, but always and everywhere "the within" determines "the beyond," and character is destiny.

V
THE ATTITUDE TOWARD THE UNSEEN

"Nowhere as yet has history spoken in favor of the ideal of a morality without religion. New active forces of will, so far as we can observe, have always arisen in conjunction with ideas about the unseen." So wrote the great German historian and philosopher, Wilhelm Dilthey. The greatest experts in the field both of ethics and of religion agree with this view. Henry Sidgwick and Leslie Stephen are experts in the field of ethics who cannot be suspected of holding a brief for religion, and yet Sidgwick says: "Ethics is an imperfect science alone. It must run up into religion to complete itself;" and Leslie Stephen says: "Morality and religion stand or fall together." Spinoza, who was denounced during his lifetime as an atheist and a destroyer of the faith, nevertheless makes love of God the whole basis of genuine ethics, insisting that there is no morality conceivable without love of God. St. Augustine's famous testimony may suffice as a religious expert's view. He says, "Love God and then you may do what you please," meaning, of course, that you cannot then approve a wrong course of action or of life.

Nowhere, certainly, are religion and ethics so wonderfully fused into one indissoluble whole as in the experience and teaching of Christ. This appears not only in His supreme rule for religion and for good conduct: "Thou shalt love God with all thy powers and thy neighbor as thyself," but still more does it appear in the inner steps and processes which underlie and prepare the way for the decisions and acts of Christ's own life. Here, unmistakably, *all the active forces of will arose in conjunction with ideas about the unseen.*

It is the modern custom to talk much about the ethics of Jesus and to see in the Sermon on the Mount an ideal of human personality and a program for an ideal social order. But a careful reader cannot fail to feel in Christ's teaching the complete fusion of His ideal for the individual and for society with His consciousness of the world of unseen realities. The new person and the new society are possible in His thought, only through unbroken *correspondence* with the world of higher forces and of perfect conditions. The only way to be perfect is to be on the way toward likeness to the heavenly Father, the only moral dynamic that will work is a love, like that of God's love, which expels all selfishness and all tendency to stop at partial and inadequate goods. If any kingdom of heavenly conditions is ever to be expected on earth, if ever we may hope for a day to dawn when the divine will is to be exhibited among men and they are to live the love-way of goodness, it is because God is our Father and we have the possibilities of His nature.

The ethical ideals of the Kingdom are inherently attached to the prayer experience of Jesus. The kind of human world which His faith builds for men is forever linked to the kind of God to whom He prays. Cut the link and both worlds fall away. We cannot shuffle the cold, hard, loveless atoms of our social world into lovely forms of coöperative relationship. The atoms must be changed. In some way we must learn how to lift men into the faith which Christ had, that God is the Father who is seeking to draw us all into correspondence with His unseen world of Life and Love. "After this manner pray ye. Our heavenly Father of the holy name, thy Kingdom come, Thy will be done on earth as it is in heaven." The two faiths make one faith—the faith in a Father-God who cares, and the faith in the realization of an ideal society based on coöperative love.

"And as He was praying, the fashion of His countenance was altered and His raiment became white and dazzling." This is a simple, synoptic account of an experience attaching to a supreme crisis of personal decision in the life of Jesus. His so-called ethics, as I have been insisting, is indivisibly bound up with His attitude toward the unseen, with His experience of a realm where what ought to be, really is. So, too, it is because He has found His inward relation with God that He makes His great decision to go forward toward Jerusalem, to meet the onset of opposition, to see His work frustrated by the rulers of the nation, to suffer and to die at the hands of His enemies. The Transfiguration has been treated as a myth and again as a misplaced resurrection story. But it is certainly best to treat it as a genuine psychological narrative which fits reality and life at every point. As the clouds darken and the danger threatens and the successful issue of His mission seems impossible, Jesus falls back upon God, brings His spirit into absolute parallelism with the heavenly will and accepts whatever may be involved in the pursuit of the course to which He is committed. When He pushes back into the inner experience of relation with His Father and the circuit of connection closes and living faith floods through Him and fixes His decision unalterably to go forward, His face and form are transfigured and illuminated through the experience of union. This prayer of illumination reported in the gospels, is not an isolated instance, a solitary experience. The altered face, the changed body, the glorified figure, the radiation of light, have marked many a subordinate saint, and may well have characterized the Master as He found the true attitude of soul toward the unseen and formed His momentous decision to be faithful unto death in His manifestation of love.

In Gethsemane, as the awful moment came nearer, once more we catch a glimpse of His attitude to the unseen. In place of illuminated form and shining garments, we hear now of a face covered with the sweat and blood of agony. Just in front are the shouting rabble, the cross and the nails, the defeat of lifelong hopes and the defection of the inner fellowship, but the triumphant spirit within Him unites with the infinite will that is steering the world and piloting all lives, and calmly acquiesces with it. But to this suffering soul, battling in the dark night of agony, the infinite will is no abstract Power, no blind fate, to be dumbly yielded to. The great word which breaks out from these quivering lips is the dear word for "Father" that the little child's lips have learned to say: "Abba." The will above is His will now and He goes forward to the pain and death in the strength of communion and fellowship with His Abba-Father. There may have been a single moment of desolation in the agony of the next day when the cry escaped, "My God, why hast thou forsaken me?" but immediately the inner spirit recovers its connection and its confidence and the crucifixion ends, as it should, with the words of triumphant faith, "Father, into thy hands I intrust my spirit."

The most important fact of this Life, which has ever since poured Alpine streams of power into the life of the world, is its attitude toward the unseen. We miss the heart of things when we reduce the gospel to ethics or when we transform it into dry theology. Through all the story and behind all the teaching is the mighty inner fact of an intimate personal *experience* of God as Father. To live is to be about the "Father's business." In great moments of intercourse there comes to Him a flooding consciousness of sonship, joyous both to Father and Son: "In Him I am well pleased," and in times of strain and tragedy the onward course is possible because the inner bond holds fast and the Abba-experience abides.

It is not strange that a synoptic writer reports the saying: "No man knoweth the Father but the Son." The passage as it stands reported in Matthew may be colored by later theology, but there is a nucleus of absolute truth hidden in the saying. There is no other way to know God but this way of inner love-experience. Only a son can know a Father. Only one who has trodden the wine-press in anguish and pain, and through it all has felt the enfolding love of an Abba-father really *knows*. Mysticism has its pitfalls and its limitations, but this much is sound and true, that the way to know God is to have inner heart's experience of Him, like the experience of the Son.

CHAPTER III
SOME PROPHETS OF THE INNER WAY

I
THE PSALMIST'S WAY

Emerson's friend, Margaret Fuller, coined the phrase, "standing the universe." "I can stand the universe," was her brave statement. But long before Concord was discovered or "the transcendental school" was dreamed of a school of Hebrew saints had learned how to stand the universe.

Canaan, with all its milk and honey, was never a land arranged by preëstablished harmony as a paradise for the idealist. It enjoyed no special millennium privileges. Whatever rainbow dreams may have filled the mind of optimistic prophets were always quickly put to flight by the iron facts of the rigid world which ringed them round. The Philistines were pitiless neighbors. Like Gawain, they were spiritually too blind even to have desires to *see*. Coats of mail, gigantic spear heads, iron chariots, and Goliath champions were their arguments. How could a nation like Israel be free to work out its spiritual career with these crude materialistic Philistines always hanging on its borders and always threatening its national existence? When the Philistines were temporarily quiet there were Moabites, or

Edomites, or Syrians ready to take a turn at hampering the ideals of Israel. And worse still was ahead. From the time of the battle of Karkar (854 B.C.) on, the armies of Assyria had to be reckoned with. Here was another pitiless foe; efficient, militant, inventive, with a culture and religion suited to its genius, but as ruthless as a wolf toward everything in its path. It smashed whatever it struck and in the course of events Jerusalem was ground in its irresistible mill.

When a "return" was granted under the Persians, and the national and religious life was restored in Jerusalem, new difficulties swarmed. During the long period of "restoration" the half-breed peoples in Palestine with their low ideals threatened to defeat the hopes of the returned exiles and made their feeble beginnings as difficult as possible. Then, again, the new nation was hardly firm in its re-found life when it had to meet the forces of Hellenism which rose out of the expansion policies of Alexander. A culture incompatible with the ideals and passions of the Hebrews broke in and surrounded them. It was a different enemy to any they had yet met but no less irreconcilable. Under the Hellenized kings of Antioch all the hopes and ideals of this long-suffering race were put in jeopardy, and the very existence of the chosen nation was in desperate peril in the period of the Maccabean struggle.

But through all these centuries of warfare with alien peoples, and during all these hard periods of strain and anguish, there existed a school of saints who were learning how to stand the universe and who were teaching the world a way of victory even in the midst of outward defeat. Their "way" was the fortification of the soul, the construction of the interior life; and the literature which they produced has proved to be one of the most precious treasures of the race. The gold dust words of these saints are scattered through most of the early books of Israel, for in all periods the poets of this race were mainly busy with this central problem of life, the problem of standing the universe. But it is in the collection which we call the *Psalms* that we find the supreme literature of this inner way of fortification and victory.

"Thou restorest my soul," is the joyous testimony of one of these saints, and this testimony of the best loved member of this school of saints is the key to the Psalmist's way of triumph in general. In the confusion of events and the irrationality of things—*die Ohnmacht der Natur*—he felt his way back, like a little child in the dark feeling for his mother, until he found God as the rock on which his feet could stand. The processes of reconstruction are never traced out. The logic of this way back to the fortification of the soul through the discovery of God is not given in detail. The moments when we shift the levels of life are never quite describable. But somehow when the way outside goes on into the valley of the shadow of death, and the table is set in the face of enemies, the soul falls back upon God and is *restored*.

"I could not understand," another Psalmist declares. Everything was baffling. The wicked seemed to prosper and the righteous to suffer. The world appeared out of joint and the whole web of life hopelessly tangled; "but," he adds with no further explanation, "I came into the sanctuary of God and then I saw." It is like the final solution in the great inner drama of Job. *God answers* and Job's problem is solved: "I had heard of thee by the hearing of the ear, but now mine eye seeth thee." In the great phrase of the book, "*God* turned the captivity of Job."

These men who gave us our Psalms had learned how to bear adversity and affliction without being overwhelmed or defeated. "All thy waves and thy billows have gone over me," one of them cries. He has lost his land and has only the *memory* of Jordan and Hermon and Mizar. His adversaries are a constant "sword in his bones." They jeer at him and ask, "Where now is thy God?" but his trust holds steadily on: "The Lord will command His loving-kindness in the daytime, and in the night His song shall be with me!" Even when the water-spouts of trouble break over him, when "the waters roar and are troubled," when the "nations rage and kingdoms are moved," when "desolations are abroad in the earth," God abides for him "a very present help in time of trouble," "a refuge and strength" for his soul. Dismay and trembling may be abroad; pain may come as on a woman in travail, yet this deep soul can calmly say, "God is our God forever; He will be our guide even unto death."

This element of *trust* and *confidence* has never anywhere had grander utterance. The Psalmist has got beyond reliance on "horses and chariots," beyond trust in "riches," "princes," in "the bow or the sword," or in "man, whose breath is in his nostrils." He rests his case on God alone, and builds on naked faith in His goodness and care: "*Thou* hast delivered my soul from death, mine eyes from tears, and my feet from falling." Puzzled he often is with the prosperity of the wicked, who "flourish like green bay-trees"; perplexed he sometimes is with God's delay in coming to the help of the poor and needy and oppressed; but his faith holds on and he does not "slide." It gives us almost a sense of awe as we see a valiant soul, hard pressed, hemmed around, deep in affliction and sorrow, "standing the world" and saying in clear voice: "Oh, give thanks unto the Lord, for He is good; His loving-kindness endureth forever!"

We understand when we read such words why this collection of Psalms has held its place in the religious life of the world. It contains the living, throbbing *experience* of great souls, who cared absolutely for one thing—to find God and to enjoy Him, and who, having found their one precious jewel, could do without all else, and by this inner experience could stand the world.

II
THE NEW AND LIVING WAY

The writer of the Epistle to the Hebrews declares that Christ has introduced into the world "a new and living way" to God. The concrete problems confronting this writer to a Jewish circle of the first century were very different from our own problems to-day, but he so succeeded in seizing an eternal aspect of the issue that his word about the new and living way is as vital now as it was then.

His "new and living way," as the tenth chapter shows, is the way of personal consecration as a substitute for the old way of sacrifice. The manner of his exposition may seem to us now a little artificial, but there can be no question of the religious significance of the conclusion. Following his usual line of interpretation, he begins by treating the great national system of sacrifices as a "shadow," *i.e.* a parable, or a figure, or a symbol, of a true and higher reality. Then he goes on boldly to declare that "sacrifices" have become empty performances—it is impossible, he says, that the blood of bulls and goats works any real change in the nature or the attitude of the soul. Next he buttresses his radical conclusion with a citation of Scripture to the effect that God has never taken pleasure in burnt offerings and ritual sacrifices, and on this Scripture text from the Psalms he rises to his new insight, that Christ has come not to do the sacrificial work of a priest, not to satisfy God by a sacrifice, but to reveal the personal power of a life of consecration: "Then said I, lo, I come to do thy will, O God." This way of dedication to the divine will, this complete consecration of self out of love for the will of God, the writer calls "the new and living way."

Two very important conclusions are inherently bound up with this transition from a religion of sacrifices to a religion of dedication. First, if carries a wholly new conception of God and secondly, it involves a complete reinterpretation of human ministry. If God does not take any pleasure in sacrifice, then the whole idea that He is a Being to be appeased by gifts, by offerings, by incense, by blood, or by self-inflicted suffering of any sort, falls to the ground. These things are not shadows or symbols; they are blunders and mistakes. The God for whom they are intended needs and asks for no such form of approach. That has always been the contention of the supreme prophets of the race, and Christ in His unveiling of God has made the fact sun-clear that God is not rightly conceived when He is thought of as needing any kind of sacrifice or any inducement to make Him forgiving or loving. Love is His nature. The new and living way leads first of all to this new revelation of God.

But no less certainly it leads to a new type of minister. The priest was conceived as an expert in ways of *satisfying* God and of *appeasing* Him. He was supposed to know what God required and how to perform the things required. He was indispensable, because only an expert, duly ordained, could do the work that was necessary for bringing God and man into relation with each other. Under "the new and living way," however, the priest has lost his occupation and the minister becomes an expert in ways of expanding human life and in bringing men to a dedication of themselves to the will of God and to the spiritual tasks of the world. In accordance with this new insight, everything that concerns religion must in some way attach to life. It must promote, or advance life, increase life, add to its height and depth, or, in some manner, make life richer and more joyous. The minister of the new and living way may be called, as he no doubt will be called, to make many sacrifices of things that are precious, and surrenders of things as dear as life itself, but there will be no inherent magic in these sacrifices. They will not be efficacious as a satisfaction to God. They will be only means toward some larger end of life, as was the case with Christ's surrenders and sacrifices. The ascetic temper will be left forever behind. Whatever is cut off, or plucked out, will be removed only for the sake of increasing the quality of life and the dynamic of it. The final test is always to be sought in the expansion of capacity, in the increase of talents, in the formation of personality, in dedication to the task of widening the area of life.

The true minister will, like the great apostle, present his body, his entire being, in living dedication. He will be satisfied with nothing short of a holy and acceptable service—acceptable, because Christlike—he will endeavor to make all his service "reasonable service"; that is, intelligent service, and he will strive earnestly not to become *set* into the mold of the world or into any deadening groove of habit, but to be *transformed* by a steady increase of life and a renewing of spiritual insight, so that he can prove what is the perfect will of God and so that he can minister to the growing life of the world.

III
AN APOSTLE OF THE INNER WAY

It is always a foolish blunder to take half when it is just as easy to have a whole, but the tendency to dichotomize all realities into halves and to assume that we are shut up to an *either-or* selection, is an ancient tendency and one that very often keeps us from winning the full richness of the life that is possible for us. Human history is strewn with dualistic formulations which have sorted men into *either-or* groups. Now it is "spirit" and "flesh" that are sharply antagonistic and men are called upon to settle which of these two halves of man's life is to have their loyalty. Again, it is "this world" and "the next world"—the here and the yonder—that bid for our heart's suffrage. "The Church" and "the world"; "faith" and "reason"; "the sacred" and "the secular" are other twin pairs that call for a sharp decision of allegiance. So, too, it has been customary to cut apart the outer life and the inner life and, with a stern *either-or*, to put them into rivalry with one another. One camp insists that religion is to be sought in deeds and effects; the other camp asserts that religion is an inward condition of life—*to be* is more important than *to do*. But this method of cutting is like that which the unnatural mother asked Solomon to perform upon the living child. It sunders what was alive and throbbing into two dead fragments, neither of which is a real half of the united living whole. In place of all the *either-or* formulations that force a choice between the halves of great spiritual realities I should put the living and undivided whole. Instead of selecting *either-or*, I prefer to take *both*. There is no line that splits the outer life and the inner life into two compartments. Nobody can *do* without *being* and nobody can *be* without *doing*. Personality is the most complete unity in the universe and it binds forever into an indissoluble and integral whole the outer and the inner, the spirit and the deed.

But at the same time it is interesting to see what a supremely great and many-sided soul like St. Paul has to say of the inwardness and interior depth of religion. That he was a man of action is plain enough to be seen and nobody can easily miss his clarion call to arm *cap-a-pie* for the positive, moral battles of life. He was ethical in the noblest sense of the word, but there was an inner core of religious experience in him which is as unique and wonderful as is his athletic ethical purpose or his imperial spirit of moral conquest.

There was for him no kind of "doing" which could ever be a substitute for the spiritual health of the soul. Nobody has ever lived who has been more deeply concerned than was St. Paul over the primary problem of life: How can my soul be saved? To be "saved" for him, however, does not mean to be rescued from dire torment or from the consequences which follow sin and dog the sinner. No transaction in another world can accomplish salvation for him; no mere change from debit to credit side in the heavenly ledgers can make him a saved man. To be saved for St. Paul is to become a new kind of person, with a new inner nature, a new dimension of life, a new joy and triumph of soul. There is a certain inner *feeling* here which systematic theology can no more convey than a botanical description of a flower can convey what the poet feels in the presence of the flower itself. There is no lack of books and articles which spread before us St. Paul's doctrines and which tell us his theory—his *gnosis*—of the plan of salvation. The trouble with all these external accounts is that they clank like hollow armor. They are like sounding brass and clanging cymbals. We miss the *real thing* that matters—the inner throbbing heart of the living experience.

What he is always trying to tell us is that a new "nature" has been formed within him, a new spirit has come to birth in his inmost self. Once he was weak, now he is strong. Once he was permanently defeated, now he is "led in a continual triumph." Once he was at the mercy of the forces of blind instinct and habit which dragged him whither he would not, now he feels free from the dominion of sin and its inherent peril to the soul. Once, with all his pride of pharisaism, he was an alien to the commonwealth of God, now he is a fellow citizen with all the inward sense of loyalty that makes citizenship real.

He traces the immense transformation to his personal discovery of a mighty forgiving love, where he had least expected to find it, in the heart of God—"We are more than conquerors through Him that loved us;" "The life I now live, I live by faith in the Son of God who loved me and gave Himself for me." *Faith*, wherever St. Paul uses it to express the central human fact of the religious life, is a word of tremendous inward depth. It is bathed and saturated with personal experience, and it proves to be a constructive life-principle of the first importance. Faith *works*; it is something by which one lives: "The life I now live, I live by faith."

But the full measure—the length and breadth, depth and height—of his new inner world does not come full into view until one sees how through faith and love this man has come into conscious relation with the Spirit of God inwardly revealed to him, and operative as a resident presence in his own spirit. No forensic account of salvation can reach this central feature of real salvation, which now appears as new inward life and power. St. Paul takes religion out of the sphere of logic into the primary region of life. There are ways of living upon the Life of God as direct and verifiable as is the correspondence between the plant and its natural environment. To *live*, in the full spiritual meaning of this word as St. Paul uses it, is to be immersed in the living currents of the circulating Life of God, and to be fed from within by those sources of creative Life which feed the evolving world: "Beholding as in a mirror the glory of the Lord, we are transformed into the same image by the Spirit of the Lord;" "He hath sent forth the Spirit of His Son into our hearts, crying Abba;" "The Spirit bears witness with our spirit that we are sons of God." With the progress of his experience and the maturing of his thought upon it, there came to St. Paul an extraordinary insight. He came to identify Christ with the Spirit: "The Lord is the Spirit." He no longer thought of Him as merely the historical person of Galilee, but rather as the eternal revelation of God, first in a definite form as Jesus the Christ, and then, after the resurrection, as

Christ the invisible Spirit, working within men, recreating and renewing their spiritual lives. The influence of Christ for salvation was, thus, with him far more than a moral influence. It was of the nature of a real energism—a spiritual power coöperating with the human will and remaking men by the formation of a new Christ-natured self within him. The process has no known or conceivable limits. Its goal is the formation of a man "after Christ": "Till Christ be formed in you." "That you may grow up into Him in all things who is the Head;" "Till we all come to the measure of the stature of the fulness of Christ." The "fruit" of the Spirit, matured in the inward realm of man's central being and expressed in common acts of daily life, is love, joy, peace, long-suffering, kindness, goodness, faithfulness, meekness, self-control—a nature in all things like that which was revealed in glory and fulness in the face of Jesus Christ.

IV
THE EPHESIAN GOSPEL

In his fresh, impressive book, *The Ephesian Gospel*, Dr. Percy Gardner says that in the early period of Christianity no city, save only Jerusalem, was more influential for the development of Christian thought than was the city of Ephesus. It was here in Ephesus, scholars are convinced, some time about the end of the first century, that the life and message of Jesus received its most sublime and wonderful interpretation, and it was through this Ephesian interpretation that the gathered mysticism of Greece and the other ancient religions of the world was indissolubly fused with the great ethical teachings of the Galilean.

It will never be known, with absolute certainty, who was the profound genius that made this Ephesian interpretation, but it will always continue to be called the gospel "according to John." There will never be any doubt, in the minds of those who read appreciatively, that, either inwardly or outwardly, the writer of it had "lain on Christ's bosom"; that he had "received of His fulness," and that he had "seen with his eyes, and heard with his ears and handled with his hands the Word of Life." He was, we can almost certainly say, one of St. Paul's men. He has fully grasped the central ideas of the apostle who first planted the truth in Ephesus, and he carries out in powerful fashion the Pauline discovery that Christ has become an invisible, eternal presence in the world. At the same time he possesses, either at first or second hand, a large amount of narrative material for the expansion of the simple gospel story as it had come from the three synoptic writers. But from first to last everything in this gospel is told for a definite purpose and every incident is loaded with a spiritual, interpretative content and meaning. He does not undervalue history or the details of the Life lived in Judea and Galilee, but he is concerned at every point to raise men's thoughts to the eternal meaning of Christ's coming, to cultivate inward fellowship with Him, and to reveal the last great *beatitude*, that those who have not seen with outward eyes, but nevertheless have *believed*, are the truly blessed ones.

The earliest of our gospel documents—the document now called Q—centers upon the "message," and gives us a collection of simple but bottomlessly profound sayings of Jesus. Another document—the gospel of Mark—hardly less primitive and no less wonderful, focuses upon the person of Jesus and His doings. Here we have in very narrow compass the earliest story of this Life, inexhaustible in its depth of love and grace, which has ever since woven itself into the very tissue of human life and thought. But now this final document, which we have been calling "the Ephesian Gospel," makes a unique contribution and carries us up to a new level of life. It announces that Jesus who gave the message, the Jesus who lived this extraordinary personal life and did the deeds of love and sacrifice, has become an ever-living, environing, permeative Spirit, continuing His revelation, reliving His life, extending His sway in men of faith. He is no longer of one date and one locality, but is present to open, responsive human hearts everywhere as the atmosphere is present to breathing lungs, or the sea to swimming fish, or the sunlight to growing plants. We can no more lose this Christ of experience than we can lose the sky.

Christianity is in this interpretation vastly more than an historical religion, bound up forever with the incidents of its temporal origin. It is as much a present fact and a present power as electricity is. It is rooted in an inexhaustible source of Life. It is as dynamic as the central springs of the universe, and it is perpetually supplied from within by invisible fountains of living energy. But this triumphant and eternal principle of the spiritual life is, "according to John," no vague, abstract principle of logic, but instead a warm, tender, intimate, concrete personification of Life, Light, and Love who has definitely incarnated the Truth and revealed the nature of God and the possible glory of man.

The great Ephesian makes no division between history and experience. The Christ of his faith and of his account is alike the Christ of history and of experience. He looks backward, and he looks inward, and the Christ of his story is the seamless and invisible product of this double process. This is wholly in the manner of the great apostle who declared "if we have known Christ after the flesh we know Him so now no more," and yet neither the Ephesian disciple nor the apostolic master discounted the importance of the facts of the Christ after the flesh. The transcendent truth for them both is the truth that the Church still has its Christ, who is leading it into all the truth and progressively revealing Himself with the expanding ages.

Every Christian mystic for nineteen hundred years has felt the influence of this great Ephesian prophet, and his message has become a part of the necessary air we breathe. His gospel and his brief epistle, loaded with its message of love, are, as Deissmann has well said, the greatest monument of the appreciation of the mystical teaching of St. Paul that has ever been reared in the world. The man who performed this immense literary task for us of the after ages now

"Lies as he lay once, breast to breast with God,"

but his *word* is still quick and powerful and he has helped us more than any other writer has done to interpret our own experience, and more than any other prophet this Ephesian has inspired our faith in the real presence and has given us the assurance, inwardly verified, that we are not comfortless and alone, in a world of pain and loss and death, but are bound as living twigs in one sap-giving Vine of Life, participants of the vitalizing, refreshing, joy-bringing bread and water of Life, and with open access to the infinite healing and comfort and fortification of the Eternal Christ.

CHAPTER IV
THE WAY OF EXPERIENCE

I
WAITING ON GOD

As worship, taken in its highest sense and widest scope, is man's loftiest undertaking, we cannot too often return to the perennial questions: What is worship? Why do we worship? How do we best perform this supreme human function? Worship is too great an experience to be defined in any sharp or rigid or exclusive fashion. The history of religion through the ages reveals the fact that there have been multitudinous ways of worshiping God, all of them yielding real returns of life and joy and power to large groups of men. At its best and truest, however, worship seems to me to be *direct, vital, joyous, personal experience and practice of the presence of God.*

The very fact that such a mighty experience as this is possible means that there is some inner meeting place between the soul and God; in other words, that the divine and human, God and man, are not wholly sundered. In an earlier time God was conceived as remote and transcendent. He dwelt in the citadel of the sky, was worshiped with ascending incense and communicated His will to beings beneath through celestial messengers or by mysterious oracles. We have now more ground than ever before for conceiving God as transcendent; that is, as above and beyond any revelation of Himself, and as more than any finite experience can apprehend. But at the same time, our experience and our ever-growing knowledge of the outer and inner universe confirm our faith that God is also immanent, a real presence, a spiritual reality, immediately to be felt and known, a vital, life-giving environment of the soul. He is a Being who can pour His life and energy into human souls, even as the sun can flood the world with light and resident forces, or as the sea can send its refreshing tides into all the bays and inlets of the coast, or as the atmosphere can pour its life-giving supplies into the fountains of the blood in the meeting place of the lungs; or, better still, as the mother fuses her spirit into the spirit of her responsive child, and lays her mind on him until he believes in her belief.

It will be impossible for some of us ever to lose our faith in, our certainty of, this vital presence which overarches our inner lives as surely as the sky does our outer lives. The more we know of the great unveiling of God in Christ, the more we see that He is a Being who can be thus revealed in a personal life that is parallel in will with Him and perfectly responsive in heart and mind to the spiritual presence. We can use as our own the inscription on the wall of the ancient temple in Egypt. On one of the walls a priest of the old religion had written for his divinity: "I am He who was and is and ever shall be, and my veil hath no man lifted." On the opposite wall, some one who had found his way into the later, richer faith, wrote this inscription: "Veil after veil have we lifted and ever the Face is more wonderful!"

It must be held, I think, as Emerson so well puts it, that there is "no bar or wall in the soul" separating God and man. We lie open on one side of our nature to God, who is the Oversoul of our souls, the Overmind of our minds, the Overperson of our personal selves. There are deeps in our consciousness which no private plumb line of our own can sound; there are heights in our moral conscience which no ladder of our human intelligence can scale; there are spiritual hungers, longings, yearnings, passions, which find no explanation in terms of our physical inheritance or of our outside world. We touch upon the coasts of a deeper universe, not yet explored or mapped, but no less real and certain than this one in which our mortal senses are at home. We cannot explain our normal selves or account for the best things we know—or even for our condemnation of our poorer, lower self—without an appeal to and acknowledgment of a divine Guest and Companion who is the real presence of our central being. How shall we best come into conscious fellowship with God and turn this environing presence into a positive source of inner power, and of energy for the practical tasks and duties of daily life?

It is never easy to tell in plain words what prepares the soul for intercourse with God; what it is that produces the consciousness of divine tides, the joyous certainty that our central life is being flooded and bathed by celestial currents. No person ever quite understands how his tongue utters its loftiest words, how his pen writes its noblest phrases, how his clearest insights came to him, how his most heroic deeds got done, or how the finest strands of his character were woven. Here is a mystery which we never quite uncover—a background which we never wholly explore lies along the fringes of the most illumined part of our lives. This mystery surrounds all the supreme acts of religion. They cannot be *reduced* to a cold and naked rational analysis. The intellect possesses no master key which unlocks all the secrets of the soul.

We can say, however, that purity of heart is one of the most essential preconditions for this high-tide experience of worship. That means, of course, much more than absence of moral impurity, freedom from soilure and stain of willful sins. It means, besides, a cleansing away of prejudice and harsh judgment. It means sincerity of soul, a believing, trusting, loving spirit. It means intensity of desire for God, singleness of purpose, integrity of heart. The flabby nature, the duplex will, the judging spirit, will hardly succeed in worshiping God in any great or transforming way.

Silence is, again, a very important condition for the great inner action which we call worship. So long as we are content to speak our own *patois*, to live in the din of our narrow, private affairs, and to tune our minds to stock broker's tickers, we shall not arrive at the lofty goal of the soul's quest. We shall hear the noises of our outer universe and nothing more. When we learn how to center down into the stillness and quiet, to listen with our souls for the whisperings of Life and Truth, to bring all our inner powers into parallelism with the set of divine currents, we shall hear tidings from the inner world at the heart and center of which is God.

But by far the most influential condition for effective worship is group-silence—the waiting, seeking, expectant attitude permeating and penetrating a gathered company of persons. We hardly know in what the group-influence consists, or why the presence of others heightens the sensitive, responsive quality in each soul, but there can be no doubt of the fact. There is some subtle telepathy that comes into play in the living silence of a congregation which makes every earnest seeker more quick to feel the presence of God, more acute of inner ear, more tender of heart to feel the bubbling of the springs of life than any one of them would be in isolation. Somehow we are able to "lend our minds out," as Browning puts it, or at least to contribute toward the formation of an atmosphere that favors communion and coöperation with God.

If this is so, if each assists all and all in turn assist each, our responsibilities in meetings for worship are very real and very great and we must try to realize that there is a form of ministry which is dynamic even when the lips are sealed.

II
IN THE SPIRIT

There has surely been no lack of discussion on the Trinity during the centuries of Christian history! But in all the welter and turmoil of words there has been surprisingly little said about the Spirit. The nature of the Father and the Son has always been the central theme, and whatever is said of the Spirit is vague and brief. The Creeds are very precise in their accounts of God the Father and of Christ the Son, but of the Spirit, they merely say without explanation or expansion: "I believe in the Holy Spirit."

The mystics and the heretics have generally had more to say of the Spirit. They have almost always claimed for themselves direct and inward guidance; they have insisted that God is near at hand, a presence to be felt, and they have endeavored to bring in a "dispensation" of the religion of the Spirit. But they, too, have contented themselves with vague and hazy accounts of the nature and operation of the Spirit. It has largely remained a subject of mystery, a kind of "fringe" with no definite idea corresponding to the word.

One reason for this haze and vagueness is due to the fact that the Spirit has generally been supposed to act suddenly, miraculously, and "as He lists," so that no law or principle or method of His operation can be discovered. He has been conceived as working upon or through the individual in such a way that the individual is merely an "instrument," receiving and transmitting what comes entirely from "beyond" himself. Consequently to be "in the Spirit" has meant to be "out of oneself," *i.e.* to be a channel for something that has had no origin in, and no assistance from, our own personal consciousness. As Philo, the famous Alexandrian teacher of the first century, states this view: "Ideas in an invisible manner are suddenly showered upon me and implanted in me by an inspiration from on high."

There is no doubt that in some cases in all ages men and women have had experiences like that of Philo's. But they are by no means universal; they are extremely rare and unusual. God does sometimes "give to His beloved in sleep" and He does apparently sometimes open the windows of the soul by sudden inrushes of light and power. It is, however, a grave mistake to limit the sphere and operation of the divine Spirit to these sudden, unusual, miraculous incursions. It is precisely that mistake—made by so many spiritual persons—that has kept Christians in general from realizing the immense importance of the work of the Spirit in everyday religious life. The mistake is, of course, due to our persistent tendency to separate the divine from the human as two independent "realities," and to treat the divine as something "away," "above," and "beyond."

St. Paul, in spite of all his rabbinical training and the dualisms of his age, is still the supreme exponent of the genuine, as opposed to the false, idea of the Spirit. Whether the sermon on the Areopagus as given in Acts is an exact report of an actual speech, or not, the words, "in Him we live and move and are," express very well St. Paul's mature conception of the all-pervasive immanence of God, though they by no means indicate the extraordinary richness and boldness of his thought. He identifies Christ and the Spirit— "the Lord is the Spirit."[2] The resurrected and glorified Christ, he holds, relives, reincarnates Himself, in Christian believers. He becomes the spirit and life of their lives. He makes through them a new body for Himself, a new kind of revelation of Himself. They themselves are "letters of Jesus Christ," written by the Spirit. He is no longer limited to one locality of the world or to one epoch of time. He is "present" wherever two or three believers meet in loyalty to Him. He is revealed wherever any of His faithful followers are working in love and devotion to extend the sway of His Kingdom. The

Church, which for St. Paul means always the fellowship of believers, living in and through the Spirit, is "a growing habitation of God."

The "sign" of the Spirit's presence is, however, no sudden miraculous bestowal like an unknown tongue or an extraordinary gift of healing. It is just a normal thing like the manifestation of love. It is proved by the increase of fellowship, the growth of group-spirit, the spread of community-loyalty. When love has come, the Spirit is there, and when love comes, those who are in its spirit suffer long and are kind; they envy not; they are not provoked; they do not exalt mistakes; they bear all things, believe all things, hope all things, endure all things. Love constructs, because it is the inherent evidence of the Spirit, living, working, operating in the persons who love. Through them the incarnation of God is continued in the world, the Spirit of Christ finds its organ of expression and life, and the Kingdom of God comes on earth as it is in heaven. This "body," this Church, this community-group of loyal believers, is "the completion of Him who through all and in all is being fulfilled."[3]

If this Pauline idea of the Spirit is the true idea—and I believe it is—then we are to look for the divine presence, the divine guidance, the divine inspiration, not so much in sudden extraordinary inrushes and miraculous bestowals, as in the processes which transform our stubborn nature, which make us loyal and loving, which bind us into fellowship with others, which form in us community-spirit and sympathetic coöperation, and which make us efficient organs of the Christ-life and of the growing Kingdom of God.

III
THE POWER OF PRAYER

It seems to me very clear that there is a native, elemental homing instinct in our souls which turns us to God as naturally as the flower turns to the sun. Apparently everybody in intense moments of human need reaches out for some great source of life and help beyond himself. That is one reason why we can pray and do pray, however conditions alter. It is further clear that persons who pray in living faith, in some way unlock reservoirs of energy and release great sources of power within their interior depths. There is an experimental energy in prayer as certainly as there is a force of gravitation or of electricity. In a recent investigation of the value of prayer, nearly seventy per cent of the persons questioned declared that they felt the presence of a higher power while in the act of praying. As one of these personal testimonies puts it: prayer makes it possible to carry heavy burdens with serenity; it produces an atmosphere of spirit which triumphs over difficulties.

It certainly is true that a door opens into a larger life and a new dimension when the soul flings itself out in real prayer, and incomes of power are experienced which heighten all capacities and which enable the recipient to withstand temptation, endure trial, and conquer obstacles. But prayer has always meant vastly more than that to the saints of past ages. It was assuredly to them a homing instinct and it was the occasion of refreshed and quickened life, but, more than that, it meant to them a time of intimate personal intercourse and fellowship with a divine Companion. It was two-sided, and not a solitary and one-sided heightening of energy and of functions. Nor was that all. To the great host of spiritual and triumphant souls who are behind us prayer was an *effective and operative power*. It accomplished results and wrought effects beyond the range of the inner life of the person who was praying. It was a way of setting vast spiritual currents into circulation which worked mightily through the world and upon the lives of men. It was believed to be an operation of grace by which the fervent human will could influence the course of divine action in the secret channels of the universe.

Is this two-sided and objective view of prayer, as real intercourse and as effective power, still tenable? Can men who accept the conclusions of science still pray in living faith and with real expectation of results? I see no ground against an affirmative answer. Science has furnished no evidence which compels us to give up believing in the reality of a personal conscious self which has a certain area of power over its own acts and its own destiny, and which is capable of intercourse, fellowship, friendship, and love with other personal selves. Science has discovered no method of describing this spiritual reality, which we call a self, nor can it explain what its ultimate nature is, or how it creatively acts and reacts in love and fellowship toward other beings like itself. This lies beyond the sphere and purview of science.

Science, again, has furnished no evidence whatever against the reality of a great spiritual universe, at the heart and center of which is a living, loving Person who is capable of intercourse and fellowship and friendship and love with finite spirits like us. That is also a field into which science has no *entrée*; it is a matter which none of her conclusions touch. Her business is to tell how natural phenomena act and what their unvarying laws are. She has nothing to say and can have nothing to say about the reality of a divine Person in a sphere within or above or beyond the phenomenal realm, *i.e.* the realm where things appear in the describable terms of space and time and causality.

Real and convincing intimations have broken into our world that there actually is a spiritual universe and a divine Person at the heart and center of it who is in living and personal correspondence with us. This is the most solid substance, the very warp and woof, of Christ's entire revelation. The universe is not a mere play of forces, nor limited to things we see and touch and measure. Above, beyond, within, or rather in a way transcending all words of space, there is a Father-God who is Love and Life and Light and Spirit, and who is as open of access to us as the lungs to the air. Nothing in our world of space disproves the truth of Christ's report. Our hearts tell us that it might be true, that it ought to be true, that it is true. And if it is true, prayer, in all the senses in which I have used it, may still be real and still be operative.

There is no doubt a region where events occur under the play of describable forces, where consequent follows antecedents and where law and causality appear rigid and unvarying. In that narrow, limited realm of space particles we shall perhaps not expect interruptions or interferences. We shall rather learn how to adjust to what is there, and to respect it as the highest will of the deepest nature and wisdom of things. But in the realm of personal relationships, in all that touches the hidden springs of life, in the stress and strain of human strivings, in the interconnections of man with man, and group with group, in the vital matters by which we live or die, in the weaving of personal and national issues and destinies, we may well throw ourselves unperplexed on God, and believe implicitly that what we pray for affects the heart of God and influences the course and current of this Deeper Life that makes the world.

IV
THE MYSTERY OF GOODNESS

We generally use the word "mystery" to indicate the dark, baffling, and forbidding aspects of our life-experience. The things which spoil our peace and mar our harmonies and break our unions are for us characteristically *mysteries*. Pain, suffering, and death are the most ancient of mysteries, which philosophers and poets have always been striving to solve and unravel. Evil in all its complicated forms and sin in all its hideous varieties constitute another group of these dark and forbidding mysteries, about which the race has forever speculated. The problem of evil has been the prolific source both of mythological stories and of systems of philosophy.

Every war that has swept the world, from that of Chedorlaomer to that of Europe to-day, has driven this mystery of evil into the foreground of consciousness, wherever the dark trail of ruin and devastation and myriad woe has lain, or lies, across the lives and hearts of men. Now, as always, burning homes, ruined business, masses of slain, maimed bodies, the welter of animal instincts, the suffering of women and little children, and the hates enflamed between races form the greatest summation of baffling evils that man has known.

But it is an interesting fact that the mysteries referred to by the greatest prophets of the soul are not of this dark and baffling type. They are mysteries of light rather than mysteries of darkness. Christ speaks of "the mystery of the Kingdom of God." Saint Paul finds the central mystery to be an incarnational revelation of a suffering, loving God, who re-lives His life in us, and the author of the Epistle to Timothy announces "the great mystery of *godliness*."[4] Love is put above all mysteries; the gospel of grace is more "unsearchable" than any suffering of this present time, and the real mystery is to be found rather in resurrection than in death: "Behold I show you a mystery. We shall not all sleep, but we shall all be changed and the dead shall be raised."

Science has confirmed this emphasis of the spiritual prophets. We come back from the greatest books of the present time with the same conclusion as this of the New Testament that the prime mysteries of the world are mysteries of goodness and not of evil; of light and not of darkness. We can pretty easily understand how there should be "evil" in a world that has evolved under the two great biological conditions: (1) Every being that survives wins out because he is more physically fit than his neighbors in the struggle for existence, and (2) there is a tendency for all inherited traits to persist in offspring. In order to have "nature" at all, there must be a heavy tinge of redness in tooth and claw. The primitive passions must be strong in order to insure any beings that can survive. And if there is to be inheritance of parental traits, then the tendencies of bygone ages are bound to persist on, even into a world of more highly evolved beings, and there will be inherited "relics" of fears, of appetites, of impulses, of instincts, and of desires, as there are inherited "relics" in the physical structure, and men will continue to do things which would better suit the animal level. And, finally, if the world is to be made by evolving processes, there will of necessity be an overlapping of "high" and "low." The world cannot *go on* without carrying its past along with the advancing line, so that in the light of the new and better that comes, the old and out-passed seems "evil" and "bad."

We can see plainly enough where the drive of selfishness came from, where the passionate fears and angers and hates that mar our world got into the system. What is not so clear and plain is how we came to be possessed of a driving hunger for *goodness*, how we ever got a bent for self-sacrifice, how we derived our disposition for love, how we discovered that it is more blessed to give than to receive. The mystery after all *is* the mystery of goodness. The gradual growth of a Kingdom of God, in which men live by love and brotherhood, in which they give without expecting returns, in which they decrease that others may increase, and in which their joy is fulfilled in the *spreading* of joy—that is, after all, the mystery.

The coming, into this checkerboard world, of One who practiced love in all the varying issues of life,

"Who nailed all flesh to the cross

Till self died out in the love of his kind,"

and who Himself believed, and taught others to believe, that His Life was a genuine revelation of God and the spiritual realm of reality—there is a mystery.

That this Life which was in Him is an actual incursion from a higher, inexhaustible world of Spirit, that we all may partake of it, draw upon it, live in it, and have it live in us, so that in some sense it becomes true that *Christ lives in us* and we are raised from the dead—that is the mystery.

This word "mystery" or "mysteries" did not, however, stand in the thought of the early Christians for something mysterious and inscrutable. It stood rather for some unspeakably precious reality which could be known only by initiation and to the initiate. The "mysteries" of Mithra were forever hidden to those on the outside; to those who formed the inner circle the secret of the real presence of the god was as open and clear as the sunlight under the sky. So, too, with the "mysteries" of the gospel. They could not be conveyed by word of wisdom or by proof of logic. Then, and always, the love of Christ "passes knowledge," "the peace of God" overtops processes of thought. Love, Grace, Goodness, Godliness, Christlikeness breaking forth in men like us, remains a "mystery"—a thing not "explainable" in terms of empirical causation and not capable of being "known" except to those who see and taste and touch, because they have been "initiated into this Life." We shall no doubt still puzzle over the dark enigmas of pain and death, of war and its train of woe, but we shall do well to remember that there is a greater mystery than any of these—the mystery of the suffering, yet ever-conquering love of God which no one *knows* except he who is immersed in it.

V
"AS ONE HAVING AUTHORITY"

The word "authority" has shifted its meaning many times. We do not mean now by it what churchmen of former times meant when they used it. Even as late as the beginning of the twentieth century a great French scholar, Auguste Sabatier, wrote an influential book in which he contrasted "Religions of Authority" with "Religions of the Spirit." By religions of authority he meant types of religion which rest on a dogmatic basis and on the super-ordinary power of ecclesiastical officials to *guarantee* the truth. However authoritative a religion of that type may once have been, it is so no longer, at least with those who have caught the intellectual spirit of our age.

"Authority" is found now for most of us where the common people who listened to Jesus found it—in the convincing and verifying power of the message itself. We should not now think for a moment of taking our views on astronomy or geology or physiology—about the circulation of the blood, for instance—on the "authority" of a priest, assuming that his ordination supplied him with oracular knowledge on these subjects. We want to know rather what the facts in any one of these fields compel us to conclude, and we go for assistance to persons who have trained and disciplined their powers of observation and who can make us see what they see. Our "authority" in the last resort to-day is the *evidence* of observable facts and legitimate *inference* from these facts. A religion of authority, then, for our generation rests, not on the infallible guarantee of any ordained man, or of any miraculously equipped church, but on the spiritual nature of human life itself and on the verifiable relations of the soul with the unseen realities of the universe.

I need hardly say—it is so plain that the runner can see it—that the so-called Sermon on the Mount is one of the best illustrations available of this type of authoritative religion. Whatever is declared as truth in that discourse is true, not because a messenger from heaven brought it, not because a supernatural authority guaranteed it, but *because it is inherently so*, and if any statement here obviously conflicted with the facts of life and stood confuted by the testimony of the soul itself, it would in the end, in the long run as we say, have to go. The whole message, from the beatitude upon the poor-in-spirit to the judgment test of life in action, as revealed in the figure of the two houses, is a message which can be verified and tried out as searchingly as can the law of gravitation or the theory of luminiferous ether. All the results that are here announced are results which attach to the essential nature of the soul, and the conditions of blessedness are as much bound up with the nature of things as are the conditions of physical health for a man, or the conditions of literary success for an author.

Any one who has read William James' chapter on "Habit" knows how it feels to be reading something which verifies itself and which convicts the judgment of the reader in almost every sentence. As one comes toward the end of the chapter he finds these words: "Every smallest stroke of virtue or of vice leaves its never so little scar. The drunken Rip Van Winkle excuses himself for every fresh dereliction by saying, 'I won't count this time!' Well! he may not count it, and a kind heaven may not count it; but it is being counted none the less. Down among the nerve cells and fibers the molecules are counting it, registering and storing it up to be used against him when the next temptation comes." These words have the irresistible drive of observable facts behind them. We have come upon *something which is so because it is so*. It can no more be juggled with or dodged than can the fact of the precession of the equinoxes. The calm authority of that chapter might well be the envy of every preacher of the gospel and of every writer of articles on religion. If either the preacher or the religious writer expects to speak to the condition of his age, then he must acquire this authoritative way of dealing with the issues of life, for the other kind of "authority" has had its day.

It is interesting to discover that Tertullian and St. Augustine—two men who, almost beyond all others, helped to forge this waning type of "authority"—came very near risking the whole case of religion in their day on the primary authority of first-hand experience and the testimony of the soul itself. "I call in," Tertullian wrote, "a new testimony; yea, one that is better known than all literature, more discussed than all doctrine, more public than all publications, greater than the whole man—I mean all which is man's. Stand forth, O soul, ... and give thy witness ... I want thy experience. I demand of thee the things thou bringest with thee into man, the things thou knowest either from thyself or from thy Author.... Whenever the soul comes to itself, as out of a surfeit or a sleep or a sickness and attains something of its natural soundness, it speaks of God."

Nobody has ever shown more skill and subtlety in examining the actual processes of the inner life than has Augustine, nor has any one more powerfully revealed the native hunger of the soul for God, or the coöperative working of divine grace in the inner region where all the issues of life are settled. Take this vivid passage, picturing the hesitating will, zig-zagging between the upward pull and the tug of the old self just before the last great act of decision which led to his conversion.

"Thus was I sick and suffering in mind, upbraiding myself more bitterly than ever before, twisting and turning in my chains in the hope that they would soon snap, for they had almost worn too thin to hold me. Yet they did still hold me. But Thou wast instant with me in the inner man, with merciful severity, redoubling the lashes of fear and shame, lest I should cease from struggling.... I kept saying within my heart, 'Let it be now, now!'—and with the word I was on the point of going on to the resolve. I had almost done it, but I had not done it; and yet I did not slip back to where I was at first, but held my footing at a short remove and drew breath. And again I tried; I came a little nearer, and again a little nearer, and now—now—I was in act to grasp and hold it; but still I did not reach it, nor grasp it, nor hold it, ... for the worse that I knew so well had more power over me than the better that I knew not, and the absolute point of time at which I was to change filled me with greater dread the more nearly I approached it."

That is straight out of life. The thing which really matters there is not some fine-spun dogma or the power of some mitered priest, but the answer of the soul, the obedience of the will in the presence of what is unmistakably divine. "The whole work of this life," he once said, "is to heal the eye of the heart by which we see God." Both these men made great contributions to the imperial, authoritative church and they were foremost architects of the immense system of dogma under which men lived for long centuries, but the religion by which they themselves lived was born in their own experience, and back of all their secondary authority was this primary authority of the soul's own testimony.

What our generation needs above everything, if I read its problems rightly, is a clearer interpretation of the spiritual capacities and the unseen compulsions of the ordinary human soul; that is to say, a more authoritative and so more compelling psychological account of the actual and potential nature of our own human self, with its amazing depths and its infinite relationships. We have had fifteen hundred years under the dogma of original sin and total depravity; now let us have a period of actually facing our own souls as they reveal themselves, not to the theologian, but to the expert in souls. We shall find them mysterious and bad enough no doubt, but we shall also find that they are strangely linked up with that unseen and yet absolutely real Heart of all things whom we call God. And our generation also needs a more authoritative account of Jesus Christ—more authoritative because more truly and more historically drawn. We have had centuries of the Christ of dogma and even to-day the Church is split and sundered by its attempt to maintain dogmatic constructions about His Person. Was He monophysite? Was he diphysite? Those dead questions have divided the world in former ages and still rally oriental sects. Our problem is different. We want to see how He lived. We want to discover what He said. We want to feel the power of His attractive personality. We want to find out what His own experience was and what bearing it has on life to-day. We need to have Him reinterpreted to us in terms of life, so that once again He becomes for us as real and as dynamic as He was for Paul in Corinth or for John in Ephesus. The moment anybody succeeds in doing *that*, He proves to be as much alive as ever, and religion becomes as authoritative as ever. Theology is not extinct, but it is becoming wholly transformed and the theology of the coming time will be a knowledge of God builded not on abstract logic, but on a penetrating psychology of man's inner nature and a no less penetrating interpretation of history and biography, especially at the points where the revelation of God has most evidently shone forth and broken in upon us.

VI
SEEING HIM WHO IS INVISIBLE

The power "to see the invisible" is as essential in science, in philosophy, in art, and in common life as it is in religion. The world with which science deals is not made out of "things that do appear." Every step in the advance of science has been made by the discovery of invisible things which explain the crude visible things of our uncritical experience. We seldom see any of the things the scientists talk about— atoms and molecules and cells, laws and causes and energies. These things have been found first, not with the eyes of sense, but with the vision of the mind.

Newton found the support that holds the earth to the sun and the moon to the earth, but there was no visible cable, no mighty grooves in which the poles of the earth's axis spin. There was nothing to see, and yet his mind discovered an invisible link that fastens every particle of matter in the universe to every other particle, however remote. One fact after another has forced the scientist to-day to draw upon an invisible world of ether for his explanations of a vast number of the things that appear. Gravitation, electrical phenomena, light and color vision, and, perhaps, the very origin of matter, are due, his mind sees, to the presence of this extraordinary world within, or behind, the world we see.

One of the greatest advances that has ever been made in the progress of medicine was made through the discovery of invisible microbes as the cause of contagious and infectious diseases. The ancients had also believed the cause of many diseases to be the presence of invisible agents, which they called "demons," but they could hit upon no way of *finding* the "demons" or of banishing them. The scientific physician "sees" the invisible microbe and he "sees" what will put this enemy *hors de combat.*

The study of philosophy is chiefly the cultivation of the power to see the invisible. Pythagoras is said to have required a period of a year of silence as an initiation into the business of philosophy—because there was nothing to talk about until the beginner had learned how to see the invisible! The great realities to which the philosopher is dedicated are not things to be found, even with microscopes or telescopes. Nobody is qualified to enter the philosophical race at all—even for the hundred-yard dash—unless in the temporal he can see the eternal, and in the visible the invisible, and in the material the spiritual. There can be no artistic creation until some one comes who has "the faculty divine" to see

"The gleam,

The light that never was, on sea or land."

Such artistic creations must not be unreal. On the contrary, they must be more real than the scenes we photograph or the factual events we describe. They must present to us something that is in all respects *as it ought to be.* The artist, the poet, the musician succeed in making some object, or some character, or some series of events or sounds raise us above our usual restraints of space and time and imperfection and for a moment give us a glimpse of something eternal.

But we see the invisible in our common daily life much more than we realize. The simple cobbler of shoes stitches and pegs at his little shoe, and makes it as honestly as he can, for some child whom he has never seen and perhaps never will see. The merchant expands his business because he forecasts the expanding need for his articles in China, Africa, or South America. The statesman at every move is dealing as much with the country of his inner vision as with the country his eyes see. So, too, is the parent as he plans for the discipline and education of his child. No one can be a good person—however simple, or however great—without leaving the things that are behind, *i.e.* the things that are actual, and going on to realize what is not yet apprehended, what exists only in forecast and vision. Religion, then, is not alone in demanding the supreme faculty of seeing the invisible. We live on all life-levels by faith, by assent to realities which are not there for our eyes. Religion only demands of us that we *see* the whole Reality which this visible fragment of nature implies, that we *see* the larger spirit which our own human spirits call for, that we *see* the eternal significance revealed in the life of Christ and in the conquests of His spirit through the ages.

CHAPTER V
A FUNDAMENTAL SPIRITUAL OUTLOOK

The most important constructive work just now laid upon us is the serious task of helping to restore faith in the actual reality of God and in the fundamental spiritual nature of our world. There is no substitute for the transforming power and inward depth which an irresistible first-hand conviction of God gives a man. Carlyle, in his usual vivid fashion, says that one man with faith in God is "stronger, not than ten men that have it not, or than ten thousand, but than *all* men that have it not!" A man can face anything when he knows absolutely that at bottom the universe is not force nor mechanism but intelligent and loving purpose, and that through the seeming confusion and welter there is a loving, throbbing, personal Heart answering back to us. The cultivation of this experience is the greatest prophetic mission laid upon the spiritual leaders of any age. Isaiah is at his fullest stature when in a fearful crisis he calls his nation from a military *alliance* with Egypt, whose people, he says, are "men and not God and whose horses are flesh and not spirit," to a *reliance* on God and on eternal resources: "In returning and rest shall ye be saved; in quietness and confidence shall be your strength." George Fox is most clearly a prophet when he reports his own experience of God: "I saw that there was an ocean of darkness and death, but that an infinite ocean of light and love flowed over the ocean of darkness. In *that* I saw the infinite love of God."

If we are to assist in the creation of a higher civilization than that against which the hand on the wall is writing "mene," we must speak of God in the present tense, we must live by truths and convictions that are grounded in our own experience, and we must endeavor to find a spiritual basis underlying all the processes of the world. Men have been living for a generation—or at least trying to live—on a naturalistic interpretation of the universe which chokes and stifles the higher spiritual life of man. We must help those who have been caught in this drift of materialism to find their way back to the spiritual meaning of the world.

We get a vivid impression of the stern and iron character of this materialistic universe from the writings of Bertrand Russell. Here are two extracts:

"Man is the product of causes which had no prevision of the end they were achieving; his origin, his growth, his hopes and fears, his loves and his beliefs, are but the outcome of accidental collocations of atoms; no fire, no heroism, no intensity of thought and feeling, can preserve an individual life beyond the grave; all the labours of the ages, all the devotion, all the inspiration, all the noonday brightness of human genius, are destined to extinction in the vast death of the solar system, and the whole temple of man's achievement must inevitably be buried beneath the débris of a universe in ruins—all these things, if not quite beyond dispute, are yet so nearly certain, that no philosophy which rejects them can hope to stand. Only within the scaffolding of these truths, only on the firm foundation of unyielding despair, can the soul's habitation henceforth be safely built."[5]

"Brief and powerless is man's life; on him and all his race the slow, sure doom falls pitiless and dark. Blind to good and evil, reckless of destruction, omnipotent matter rolls on its relentless way; for Man, condemned to-day to lose his dearest, to-morrow himself to pass through the gate of darkness, it remains only to cherish, ere yet the blow falls, the lofty thoughts that ennoble his little day; disdaining the coward terrors of the slave of Fate, to worship at the shrine that his own hands have built; undismayed by the empire of chance, to preserve a mind free from the wanton tyranny that rules his outward life; proudly defiant of the irresistible forces that tolerate, for a moment, his knowledge and his condemnation, to sustain alone, a weary but unyielding Atlas, the world that his own ideals have fashioned despite the trampling march of unconscious power."[6]

Much of the present confusion has been due to a false interpretation of the doctrine of evolution. It has been assumed—not indeed by scientists of the first rank, but by a host of influential interpreters—that the basis of evolution, the law which runs the cosmic train, is competitive struggle for existence, that is to say the natural selection of the fittest to survive, and the fittest on this count are of course the physically fittest, the most efficient. This principle, used first to explain biological development, has been taken up and expanded and used to explain all ethical and social progress. Any nation that has won out and prevailed has done so, on this theory, because it made itself stronger than those nations with which it competed. This theory has contributed immensely toward bringing on the catastrophe in Europe. It is a breeder of racial rivalries, it is loaded with emotional stress, it cultivates fear, one of the main causes of war, and it runs on all fours with materialism.

But it does not fit the facts of life and it is as much a mental construction and as untrue to the complete nature of things as were the popular pre-evolution theories. Here, as everywhere else, the truth is the only adequate remedy, and the truth would set men free. Biologists of the most eminent rank have all along been insisting that life has not evolved through the operation of one single factor; for example, the law of competing struggle. Everywhere in the process, from lowest to highest, there has been present the operation of another force as primary as the egoistic factor, namely the operation of mutual aid, coöperation, struggle for the life of others, mother-traits and father-traits, sacrifice of self for the group, a love-factor implicit at the bottom but gloriously conscious and consecrated at the top. Nature has always been forerunning and crying in the wilderness that the way of *love* will work.

It is impossible to account for a continuously progressive evolution on any mechanical basis. As soon as life appeared there came into play some degree of spontaneity, something unpredictable; something which is not mechanism. The future in any life-series is never an equation with the past. What has been, does not quite determine what will be. Life carries in itself a creative tendency—a tendency to exhibit surprises, novelties, variations, mutations, unpredictable leaps. We can name this tendency, this upward-changing drive, "vital impulse," but however we name it, we cannot explain it. The variation which raises the entire level of life is as mysterious as a virgin birth, or a resurrection from the dead. There is no help in the word "fortuitous," or "accidental," there is no answer when the appeal is made either to heredity or to physical environment. There is in favorable mutations a revelation of some kind of intelligent push, a power of life working toward an end. The end or goal of the process seems to be an operative factor *in* the process. Evolution seems to be due to a mighty living, conscious, spiritual driving force, that is pouring itself forth in ever-heightening ways of manifestation and that differentiates itself into myriad varieties of form and activity, each one with its own peculiar potency of advance. Consciousness, in Henri Bergson's illuminating interpretation of evolution, is the original creative cosmic force. It is before matter, and its onward destiny is not bound up with matter. Wherever it appears there is vital impulse, upward-pointing mutations, free action, and potency. But no life is isolated or cut apart. Each particular manifestation of life is one of the rills into which the immense river of consciousness divides, and this irresistible river with its onward leaps seems able to beat down every resistance and clear away the most formidable obstacles—perhaps even death itself.

But it is not merely in the evolutionary process that we need to reinterpret the spiritual factor; it is urgently called for in our dealing with the whole of nature. We must learn how to interpret the fundamental spiritual implications involved in the nature of beauty, of moral goodness, of verifiable knowledge, and of personality itself.

In an impressive way Arthur Balfour in his *Theism and Humanism* has pointed out that it is impossible to find any adequate rational basis for our experience of beauty, or for our pursuit of moral ends of goodness, or for our confidence in the validity of knowledge or truth, unless we assume the reality of an underlying spiritual universe as the root and ground both of nature without us and of mind within us. "Æsthetic values," Balfour says, "are in part dependent upon a spiritual conception of the world in which we live."[7] "Ethics," again he says, "must have its roots in the divine; and in the divine it must find its consummation"[8] and, finally, he says that if rational values are to remain undimmed and unimpaired, God must be treated as real—"He is Himself the condition of scientific knowledge."[9]—"We must hold that reason and the works of reason have their source in God: that from Him they draw their inspiration, and that if they repudiate their origin, by this very act they proclaim their own insufficiency."[10]

Personality carries in all its larger aspects inevitable implications of a spiritual universe. In the first place, it is forever utterly impossible to find a materialistic or naturalistic *origin* for personality. Whenever we deal with "matter" or with "nature," consciousness is always presupposed, and the "matter" we talk about, or the "nature" we talk about, is "matter" or "nature" as existing for consciousness or as conceived by consciousness. It is impossible to get any world at all without a uniting, connecting principle of consciousness which binds fact to fact, item to item, event to event, into a whole which is known to us through the action of our organizing consciousness. Since it is through consciousness that a connected universe of experience is possible it seems absurd to suppose that consciousness is a product of matter or of any natural, mechanical process. Every effort to find a genesis of knowledge in any other source than spirit, derived in turn from self-existing Spirit, has always failed and from the logical nature of the case must fail. There is no answer to the question, how did we begin to be persons? which does not refer the genesis to an eternal spiritual Principle in the universe, transcending space and time, life and death, matter and motion, cause and effect—a Principle which itself is the condition of temporal beginnings and temporal changes or ends.

Normal human experience is, too, heavily loaded with further inevitable implications of an environing spiritual world. The consciousness of finiteness with which we are haunted presupposes something infinite already in consciousness, just as our knowledge of "spaces" presupposes *space*, of which definite spaces are determinate parts. That we are oppressed with our own littleness, that we revolt from our meannesses, that we "look before and after, and sigh for what is not," that we are never satisfied with any achievement, that each attainment inaugurates a new drive, that we feel "the glory of the imperfect," means that in some way we partake of an infinite revealed in us by an inherent necessity of self-consciousness. We are made for something which does not yet appear, we are inalienably kin to the perfect that always draws and attracts us. We are forever seeking God because, in some sense, however fragmentary, we have found Him.

"Here sits he shaping wings to fly;

His heart forbodes a mystery:

He names the name Eternity.

"That type of Perfect in his mind

In Nature can he nowhere find.

He sows himself on every wind.

"He seems to hear a heavenly Friend,

And through thick veils to apprehend

A labor working to an end."[11]

The most august thing in us is that creative center of our being, that autonomous citadel of personality, where we form for ourselves ideals of beauty, of truth, and of goodness by which we live. This power to extend life in ideal fashion is the elemental moral fact of personal life. These ideals which shape our life are manifestly things which cannot be "found" anywhere in our world of sense experience. They are not on land or sea. We live, and, when the call for it comes, we joyously *die* for things which our eyes have never seen in this world of molecular currents, for things which are not here in the world of space, but which are not on that account any less *real*. We create, by some higher drive of spirit, visions of *a world that ought to be* and these visions make us forever dissatisfied with *the world that is*, and it is through these visions that we reshape and reconstruct the world which is being made. The elemental spiritual core in us which we call conscience can have come from nowhere but from a deeper spiritual universe with which we have relations. It cannot be traced to any physical origin. It cannot be reduced to any biological function. It cannot be explained in utilitarian terms. It is an august and authoritative loyalty of soul to a Good that transcends all goods and which will not allow us to substitute prudence for intrinsic goodness. This inner imperative overarches our moral life, and it rationally presupposes a spiritual universe with which we are allied.

There is, too, an immense interior depth to our human personality. Only the surface of our inner self is lighted up and is brought into clear focal consciousness. There are, however, dim depths underlying every moment of consciousness and these subterranean deeps are all the time shaping or determining the ideas, emotions, and decisions which surge up into the illuminated apex of consciousness. This submerged life is in part, no doubt, the slow deposit of previous experiences, the gathered wisdom of the social group in which we are imbedded, the residual savings from unuttered hopes and wishes, aspirations and intentions,

"All I could never be,

All, men ignored in me."

But at times our interior deep seems to be more than a deposit of the past. Incursions from beyond our own margin seem to occur. Inrushes from a wider spiritual world seem to take place. Vitalizing, energizing, constructive forces come from somewhere into men, as though another universe impinged upon our finite spirits. We cannot *prove* by these somewhat rare and unusual mystical openings that there is an actual spiritual environment surrounding our souls, but there are certainly experiences which are best explained on that hypothesis, and there is no good reason for drawing any impervious boundary around the margins of the spiritual self within us.

All attempts to reduce man's inner spiritual life to the play of molecular forces have fallen through. Correlation between mind and brain cortex there certainly is and spirit, as we know it, expresses itself under, or in relation to, certain physical conditions. But it is impossible to establish a complete parallelism between mind-functions and brain-functions. The psychical, that is to say spirit, seems immensely to outrun its organ and to use brain as a musician uses an instrument.

The psychological studies of Henri Bergson in France and of Dr. William McDougall at Oxford make a very strong argument for the view that the higher forms of consciousness cannot be explained in terms of brain action and that there is no well-defined physical correlate to the highest and most central psychical processes. I shall follow in the main the positions of my old teacher, Dr. McDougall, as worked out in his *Body and Mind*.

One of the most important differences between human and animal consciousness comes to light in the appearance of "meaning" which is a differentiating characteristic of *personal* consciousness. We pass "a great divide" when we pass from bare sensory experience, common to all higher animals, to *consciousness of "meaning,"* which is a trait common only to persons. We all know what it is to hear words which make a clear impression and which yet arouse no "meaning." We often gaze at objects and yet, like Macbeth, have "no speculation in our eyes"—we apprehend no significant "meaning" in the thing upon which we are looking. We sometimes catch ourselves in the very act of passing from mere sense or bare image to the higher level of "meaning." While we gaze or while we listen we suddenly feel the "meaning" flood in and transform the whole content of consciousness. All the higher ranges of experience depend on this unique feature which is something over and above the mere sensory stage. The words, "the quality of mercy is not strain'd" remain just word-sounds until in a flash one sees that mercy is "not something that comes out grudgingly in drops," and then the mind rises to "a consciousness of meaning."[12] In this higher experience, "meaning" stands vividly in the focus of consciousness and, in a case, for instance, of grasping a long sentence, or of appreciating a piece of music, consciousness of "meaning" is an integral unitary whole. Now there is no corresponding unitary whole in the brain which could stand as the physical correlate to this consciousness of "meaning." The simple sensational experiences correspond in some way to parallel brain processes but these elemental experiences are merely cues which evoke higher forms of psychical "meaning," that have no physical or mechanical correlate in the brain.

This is still more strikingly the case in the higher forms of memory. The lower and more mechanical forms of memory may be treated as a habit-sequence, linked up with permanent brain paths. But memory proper depends, as does "meaning," upon a single act of mental apprehension. As McDougall well says: "the whole process and effect, the apprehension and the retention and the remembering, are absolutely unique and distinct from all other apprehensions and retentions and rememberings."[13] The higher kind of memory involves "meaning" and, the moment "meaning" floods in, vast and complicated wholes of experience tend to become a permanent possession, while only with multitudinous repetitions can we fix and keep processes that are meaningless and without psychical significance. But here once more this higher unitary consciousness of a remembered whole of experience has no assignable physical correlate in the brain-processes. Certain sensory cues evoke or recall a synthetic whole of consciousness which has no parallel in the material world.

Still more obviously in the higher æsthetic sentiments and volitional processes is there a spiritual activity which transcends the mechanical and physical order. Æsthetic joy depends upon a spiritual power to combine many elements of experience to form an object of a higher order than any object given to sense. It is particularly true of the highest æsthetic joy, for example, enjoyment of poetic creations where the ideal and intellectual element vastly overtops the sensuous, and where the words and imagery really carry the reader on into another world than the one of sight and sound. Here in a very high degree we attain a unified whole of consciousness that has no physical correlate among the brain-processes. It is further apparent that the higher forms of pleasure somehow exert an effective influence upon the physical system itself as though some new and heightening energy poured back from consciousness into the cerebral processes and drained down through the system. William James has given a very successful account of the way in which pleasure and pain as spiritual energies reinforce or damp the physical activities, so that the personal soul seems to take a unique part from within in determining the physical process. Here are his words:

"Tremendous as the part is which pleasure and pain play in our psychic life, we must confess that absolutely nothing is known of their cerebral conditions. It is hard to imagine them as having special centres; it is harder still to invent peculiar forms of process in each and every centre, to which these feelings may be due. And let one try as one will to represent the cerebral activity in exclusively mechanical terms, I, for one, find it quite impossible to enumerate what seem to be the facts and yet to make no mention of the psychic side which they possess. However it be with other drainage currents and discharges, the drainage currents and discharges of the brain are not purely physical facts. They are *psycho-physical* facts, and the spiritual quality of them seems a codeterminant of their mechanical effectiveness. If the mechanical activities in a cell, as they increase, give pleasure, they seem to increase all the more rapidly for that fact; if they give displeasure, the displeasure seems to damp the activities. The psychic side of the phenomenon thus seems somewhat like the applause or hissing at a spectacle, to be an encouraging or adverse *comment* on what the machinery brings forth."[14]

The unifying effect and the dynamic quality of a persistent resolution of will is another case in point which seems to show that the psychical reality in us vastly overtops the mechanism through which it works. A fixed purpose, a moral ideal, a determined intention, work far-reaching results and in some way organize and reinforce the entire nervous mechanism. The whole phenomenon of *attention* which has a primary importance for decisions of will and immense bearing on the problem of freedom of will is something which cannot be worked out in brain-terms. There seems to be some unifying central psychical core within us that raises us out of the level of mechanism and makes us autonomous creative beings. Once more I quote William James, whom many of us of this generation revere both as teacher and friend:

"It often takes effort to keep the mind upon an object. We feel that we can make more or less of effort as we choose. If this feeling be not deceptive, if our effort be a spiritual force, and an indeterminate one, then of course it contributes coequally with the cerebral conditions to the result. Though it *introduce* no new idea, it will deepen and prolong the stay in consciousness of innumerable ideas which else would fade more quickly away. The delay thus gained might not be more than a second in duration—but that second may be *critical*; for in the constant rising and falling of considerations in the mind, where two associated systems of them are nearly in equilibrium it is often a matter of but a second more or less of attention at the outset, whether one system shall gain force to occupy the field and develop itself, and exclude the other, or be excluded itself by the other. When developed, it may make us act; and that act may seal our doom. The whole drama of the voluntary life hinges on the amount of attention, slightly more or slightly less, which rival motor ideas receive. But the whole feeling of reality, the whole sting and excitement of our voluntary life, depends on our sense that in it things are *really being decided* from one moment to another, and that it is not the dull rattling off of a chain that was forged innumerable ages ago. This appearance, which makes life and history tingle with such a tragic zest, *may* not be an illusion. Effort may be an original force and not a mere effect, and it may be indeterminate in amount."[15]

There are thus a number of modes of consciousness, and I have mentioned only a few of them, which have no traceable counterpart in the physical sphere, and which presuppose a spiritual reality at the center of our personal life, and this spiritual reality, as we have seen, can trace its origin only to a self-existing, self-explanatory, environing consciousness, sufficiently personal to be the source of our developing personality. If this view is correct and sound, there is no scientific argument against the continuation of life after death. If personality is fundamentally a spiritual affair and the body is only a medium and organ here in space and time of a psychical reality, there are good grounds and solid hopes of permanent conservation.

But after all the supreme evidence that the universe is fundamentally spiritual is found in the revelation of personal life where it has appeared at its highest and best in history, that is in Jesus Christ. In Him we have a master manifestation of that creative upward tendency of life, a surprising mutation, which in a unique way brought into history an unpredictable inrush of life's higher forces. The central fact which concerns us here is that He is the revealing organ of a new and higher order of life. We cannot appropriate the gospel by reducing it to a doctrine, nor by crystallizing it into an institution, nor by postponing its prophesies of moral achievement to some remote world beyond the stars. We can appropriate it only when we realize that this Christ is a revelation here in time and mutability of the eternal nature and character of that conscious personal Spirit that environs all life and that steers the entire system of things, and that He has come to bring us all into an abundant life like His own. Here in Him the love-principle which was heralded all through the long, slow process has come into full sight and into full operation as the way of life. He shows us the meaning and possibility of genuine spiritual life. He makes us sure that His kind of life is divine, and that in His face we are seeing the heart and mind and will of God. Here at least is one place in our mysterious world where love breaks through—the love that will not let go, the love that suffers long and is kind. He makes the eternal Father's love visible and vocal in a life near enough to our own to move us with its appeal and enough beyond us to be forever our spiritual goal. We have here revealed a divine-human life which we can even now in some measure live and in which we can find our peace and joy, and through which we can so enter into relation with God that life becomes a radiant thing, as it was with Him, and death becomes, as with Him, a way of going to the Father.

CHAPTER VI
WHAT DOES RELIGIOUS EXPERIENCE TELL US ABOUT GOD

"A noiseless, patient spider,

I mark'd, where, on a little promontory, it stood, isolated;

Mark'd how, to explore the vacant, vast surrounding,

It launch'd forth filament, filament, filament, out of itself;

Ever unreeling them—ever tirelessly speeding them.

"And you, O my Soul, where you stand,

Surrounded, surrounded, in measureless oceans of space,

Ceaselessly musing, venturing, throwing,—seeking the spheres, to connect them;

Till the bridge you will need, be form'd—till the ductile anchor hold;

Till the gossamer thread you fling, catch somewhere, O my soul."—WALT WHITMAN.

There are many forms of experience which in the primary, unanalyzed, unreflective stage appear to bring us into immediate contact with self-transcending reality. We seem to be nearer the heart of things, more imbedded in life and in reality itself when consciousness is fused and unified in an undifferentiated whole of experience than in the later stage of reflection and description. This later stage necessarily involves reduction because it involves abstraction. We cannot bring any object or any experience to exact description without stripping it of its life and its mystery and without reducing it to the abstract qualities which are unvarying and repeatable.

There can be no doubt that our experiences of beauty, for instance, have a physical and describable aspect. The sunset which thrills us is for descriptive purposes an aggregation of minute water-drops which set ether waves vibrating at different velocities, and, as a result, we receive certain nerve shocks that are pleasurable. These nerve shocks modify brain cells and affect arterial and visceral vibrations, all of which might conceivably be accurately described. But no complete account of these minute cloud particles, or of these ether vibrations; no catalogue of these nerve shocks, cell changes, or arterial throbs can catch or present to us what we get in the naïve and palpitating experience of beauty itself. Something there in the field of perception has suddenly fused our consciousness into an undifferentiated whole in which sensuous elements, intellectual and ideal elements, emotional and conative elements are indissolubly merged into a vital *system* which baffles all analysis. Something got through perception puts all the powers of the inner self into play and into harmony, overcomes all dualisms of self and other, annuls all contradictions that may later be discovered, lifts the mind to the apprehension of objects of a higher order than that of sense, and liberates and vitalizes the soul with a consciousness of possession and joy and freedom.

The flower of the botanist is an aggregation of ovary, calyx, petals, pistil, and pollen—a thing which can be exactly analyzed and described. The poet's flower, on the other hand, is never a flower which could be pressed in a book or dried in an herbarium. It is a tiny finite object which suddenly opens a glimpse into a world which mere sense-eyes never see. It gives "thoughts that do lie too deep for tears." It is something so bound in with the whole of things that if one understood it altogether, he would know "what God and man is."

These experiences, even if they do not *prove* that there is a world of a higher order than that of mechanism and causal systems, at least bring the recipient moments of relief when he no longer cares for proof and they enable him to feel that he has authentic tidings of a world which is as it ought to be.

Our world of "inner experience" can in a similar way be dealt with by either one of these two characteristically different methods of approach. We can say, if we wish to do so, as Professor Leuba does in his *Psychology of Religion*, that "inner experience belongs entirely to psychology," "the conscious life belongs entirely to science,"[16] "we must deal with inner experience according to the best scientific methods;"[17] or we can seize by an interior integral insight the rich concrete *meaning* and significance of the unanalyzed whole of consciousness, as it lives and moves in us.

Psychology, like all sciences, proceeds by analysis and limitation. It breaks up the integral whole of inner experience. It strips away all mystery, all that is private and unique, and it selects for exact description the permanent and repeatable aspects, and ends with a consciousness which consists of "mind-states," or describable "contents." Everything that will not reduce to this scientific "form" is ousted from the lists as negligible. All independent variables, all aspects of "meaning," all will-attitudes, the unique feature of personal ideals, the integral consciousness of self-identity, the inherent tendency to transcend the "given"—all these features are either ignored or explained in terms of substitutes. Psychology confines itself, and must confine itself, to an empirical and describable order of facts. It could no more discover a transcendent world-order than could geology or astronomy. Its field is phenomena and the "man" it reports upon is "a naturalistic man," as completely describable as the sunset cloud or the botanist's flower.

What I insist upon, however, is that this "described, naturalistic man" is not a real existing, living, acting man possessed of interior experience. He is a constructed man. No addition of described "mind-states," no summation of "mind-contents" would ever give consciousness in its inner living wholeness. The reality whose presence makes all the difference may be named "fringe," or "connecting principle," or "synthetic unity" or anything you please—"but oh! the difference to me!" The "psychic elements" of the psychologist are never really *parts*. Every psychical state is in reality what it is because it belongs to a person, is flooded with unique life, and is imbedded in a peculiar whole of personality. Forever psychology by its method of analysis misses, and must miss, the central core of the reality. It can analyze, reduce, and describe the abstract, universal, and repeatable aspects, but it cannot catch the thing itself any more than a cinematograph can.

Here in the inner life, if anywhere, we are justified in seizing and valuing the unified and undifferentiated whole of experience in its central meaning. If this primary experience of integral wholeness and unity of self be treated as an illusion, to what other pillar and ground of truth can we fasten? The object of beauty always reveals to us something which must be comprehended as a totality greater than the sum of its parts. The thing of beauty takes us beyond the range of the method of description. So, too, in the case of our richest, most intense, and unified moments of inner consciousness, we cannot get an adequate account by the method of analysis. We must supplement science by the best testimony we can get of the worth and meaning and implications of interior insight. We must get, where possible, appreciative accounts of the undifferentiated and unreduced experience and then we can raise the question as to what is rationally involved in such personal experiences.

As mystical experience supplies us with moments of the highest integral unity, the richest wholes of consciousness, I shall deal mainly with that type, and I shall endeavor to see whether it gives any proof of a trans-subjective reality. There can be no doubt that this type of experience brings the recipient spiritual holidays from strain and stress, that it gives life an optimistic tone, and leaves behind a fresh supply of energy to live by, but can it carry us any farther? Does it supply us with a ladder or a bridge by which we can get "yonder"?

Josiah Royce in *The World and the Individual* says that the mystic "gets his reality not by thinking, but by consulting the data of experience. He is trying very skillfully to be a pure empiricist." "Indeed," he adds, "I should maintain that the mystics are the only thoroughgoing empiricists in the history of philosophy."[18] "Finite as we are," Royce says elsewhere in the same book, "lost though we may seem to be in the woods or in the wide air's wilderness, in the world of time and chance, we have still, like the strayed animals or like the migrating birds, our homing instinct."[19]

Now the mystics in all ages have insisted that, whether the process be named "instinct," or "intuition," or "inner sense," or "uprushes," the spirit of man is capable of immediate experience of God. There is something in man, "a soul-center" or "an apex of soul," which directly apprehends God. It is an immense claim, but those who have the experience are as sure that they have found a wider world of life as is the person who thrills with the appreciation of beauty.

Cases of the experience are so well known to us all to-day that I shall quote only a very few accounts. It looks to me as though some of this direct and immediate experience underlay the entire fabric of St. Paul's transforming and dynamic religious life. "It pleased God to reveal His Son in me." "It is no longer I that live but Christ liveth in me." "God sent forth the Spirit of His Son into our hearts, crying *Abba*, Father." "God who commanded the light to shine out of darkness hath shined in our hearts." The entire autobiographical story, wherever it comes into light, lets us see a man who is able to face immense tasks and to die daily because he feels in some real way that his life has become "a habitation of God through the Spirit" and that he is being "filled to all fullness with God." St. Augustine in the same way makes the reader of the *Confessions* feel that the most wonderful thing about this strange African who was for a thousand years to be the Atlas, on whose shoulders the Church rested, was his experience of God. He is speaking out of experience when he says, "My God is the Life of my life." "Thou, O God, hast made us for Thyself and our hearts are restless until they rest in Thee." "I tremble and I burn; I tremble feeling that I am unlike Him; I burn feeling that I am like Him." "I heard God as the heart heareth." "We climbed in inner thought and speech, and in wonder of Thy works, until we reached our own minds and passed beyond them and touched That which is not made but is now as it ever shall be, or rather in It is neither 'hath been' nor 'shall be' but only 'is'—just for an instant touched It and in one trembling glance arrived at That which is."

Jacob Boehme's testimony is very familiar, but it is such a good interior account that I must repeat it.

"While I was in affliction and trouble, I elevated my spirit, and earnestly raised it up unto God, as with a great stress and onset, lifting up my whole heart and mind and will and resolution to wrestle with the love and mercy of God and not to give over unless He blessed me—then the Spirit did break through. When in my resolved zeal I made such an assault, storm, and onset upon God, as if I had more reserves of virtue and power ready, with a resolution to hazard my life upon it, suddenly my spirit did break through the Gate, not without the assistance of the Holy Spirit, and I reached to the innermost Birth of the Deity, and there I was embraced with love as a bridegroom embraces his bride. My triumphing can be compared to nothing but the experience in which life is generated in the midst of death or like the resurrection from the dead. In this Light my spirit suddenly saw through all, and in all created things, even in herbs and grass, I knew God—who He is, how He is, and what His will is."[20]

Very impressive are the less well-known words of Isaac Penington: "This is He, this is He: There is no other. This is He whom I have waited for and sought after from my childhood. I have met with my God; I have met with my Savior. I have felt the healings drop into my soul from under His wings."[21]

Edward Carpenter has given many accounts of the transforming experience when he felt himself united in a living junction with the infinite "including Self." "The prince of love," he says, "touched the walls of my hut with his finger from within, and passing through like a great fire delivered me with unspeakable deliverance."[22] It brought him, as he himself says, "an absolute freedom from mortality accompanied by an indescribable calm and joy."[23] A nameless writer in the "Atlantic Monthly" for May, 1916, has given a remarkable description of an experience which is called "Twenty Minutes of Reality." "I only remember," the writer says, "finding myself in the very midst of those wonderful moments, beholding life for the first time in all its young intoxication of loveliness in its unspeakable joy, beauty, and importance. I cannot say what the mysterious change was—I saw no new thing, but I saw all the usual things in a miraculous new light—in what I believe is their true light.... Once out of all the gray days of my life I have looked into the heart of reality; I have witnessed the truth; I have seen life as it really is—ravishingly, ecstatically, madly beautiful, and filled to overflowing with a wild joy and a value unspeakable."

Finally, I shall give a modern Russian writer's appreciative report of a typical mystical experience:

"There are seconds when you suddenly feel the presence of the eternal harmony perfectly attained. It's something not earthly—I don't mean in the sense that it's heavenly—but in that sense that man cannot endure it in his earthly aspect. He must be physically changed or die. This feeling is clear and unmistakable; it's as though you apprehend all nature and suddenly say, 'Yes, that's right.' God, when He created the world, said at the end of each day of creation, 'Yes, it's right, it's good.' It ... it's not being deeply moved, but simply joy. You don't forgive anything because there is no more need of forgiveness. It's not that you love—oh, there's something in it higher than love—what's most awful is that it's terribly clear and such joy. In those five seconds I live through a lifetime, and I'd give my whole life for them, because they are worth it."[24]

It should always be noted that the number of persons who are subject to mystical experiences—that is to say, persons who feel themselves brought into contact with an environing Presence and supplied with new energy to live by—is much larger than we usually suppose. We know only the mystics who were dowered with a literary gift and who could tell in impressive language what had come to them, but of the multitude of those who have felt and seen and who yet were unable to tell in words about their experience, of these we are ignorant. An undeveloped and uncultivated form of mystical consciousness is present, I think, in most religious souls, and whenever it is unusually awake and vivid the whole inner and outer life is intensified by such experiences, even though there may be little that can be put into explicit account in language. There are multitudes of men and women now living, often in out-of-the-way places, in remote hamlets or on isolated farms, who are the salt of the earth and the light of the world in their communities, because they have had vital experiences that revealed to them realities which their neighbors missed and that supplied them with energy to live by which the mere "church-goers" failed to find.

I am more and more convinced, as I pursue my studies on the meaning and value of mysticism, with the conviction that religion, *i.e.* religion when it is real, alive, vital, and transforming, is essentially and at bottom a mystical act, a direct response to an inner world of spiritual reality, an implicit relationship between the finite and infinite, between the part and the whole. The French philosopher, Émile Boutroux, has finely called this junction of finite and infinite in us, by which these mystical experiences are made possible, "the Beyond that is within"—"the Beyond," as he says, "with which man comes in touch on the inner side of his nature."

Whenever we go back to the fundamental mystical experience, to the soul's first-hand testimony, we come upon a conviction that the human spirit transcends itself and is environed by a spiritual world with which it holds commerce and vital relationship. The constructive mystics, not only of the Christian communions but also those of other religions, have explored higher levels of life than those on which men usually live, and they have given impressive demonstration through the heightened dynamic quality of their lives and service that they have been drawing upon and utilizing reservoirs of vital energy. They have revealed a peculiar aptitude for correspondence with the Beyond that is within, and they have exhibited a genius for living by their inner conviction of God, "of practicing God," as Jeremy Taylor called it.

But are we justified in making such large affirmations? Is there anything in the nature of mystical experience that warrants us in taking the leap from inner vision to existential reality? Can we legitimately get from a finite, subjective feeling to an objective and infinite God? The answer is of course obvious. There is no way to get a bridge from finite to infinite, from subject to object, from *idea* to that which the idea *means*, from human to divine, from mere man to God, if they are isolated, sundered, disparate entities to start with. No mere finite experience of a mere finite thing can be anything but finite, and no juggling can get out of the experience what is not in it. If we mean by "empirical" that which is "given" as explicit sense-content of consciousness, then the only empirical argument that could be would be the statement that we experience what we experience. We should not get beyond the consciousness of interjection—"lo!" "voila!"

In this sense of the term, of course nobody ever did or ever could "experience God." We are shut up entirely to a stream of inner states, a seriatim consciousness, "a shower of shot," which can give us no *knowledge* at all, either, in Berkeley's words, of "the choir of heaven" or of "the furniture of earth" or of "the mighty frame of the world," or in fact, of any permanent self within us.

Used in the narrow Humian sense there are no "empirical arguments" for the existence of God, but the misery of it is there are no arguments for anything else either! We must therefore widen out the meaning of the term "empirical" and include in it not only the actual "content" of experience, but all that is involved and implicated *in* experience. We cannot talk about any kind of reality until we interpret experience through its rational implications. Nobody ever perceives "a black beetle" and knows it as "a black beetle" without transcending "pure empiricism," *i.e.* without using categories which are not a product of experience. All experience which has any knowledge-import, or value, possesses within itself self-transcendence, that is to say, it apprehends or takes by storm some sort of external or objective reality. Nobody is ever disturbed by the fallacy of subjectivism until he has become debauched by metaphysics. The fallacy of subjectivism is always the product of the abstract intellect, *i.e.* the intellect which divides experience, and takes an abstract part for a whole.

It is further true that all knowledge-experience possesses within itself finite-transcendence, *i.e.* it contains in itself a principle of infinity and could become absolutely rationalized only in an infinite whole of reality with which the experience is in organic unity. I agree fully with Professor Hocking that "it is doubtful whether there are any finite ideas at all." The consciousness of the finite has working in it the reality of the whole. The finite can never be considered as self-existent; it can never be real. There is forever present in the very heart and nature of consciousness a trope, a nisus, a straining of the fragment to link itself up with the self-complete whole, and every flash of knowledge and every pursuit of the good reveals that *trend*. Something of the *other* is always in the *me*—and however finite I may be I am always beyond myself, and am conjunct with "the pulse beat of the whole system." Either we must give up talking of knowledge or we must affirm that knowledge involves a self-complete and self-explanatory reality with which our consciousness has connection. We cannot think finite and contingent things, or aim at goodness however fragmentary, without rational appeal to something infinite and necessary. Human experience cannot be rationally conceived except as a fragment of a vastly more inclusive experience, always implied within the finite spirit, unifying and binding together into one whole all that is absolutely real and true. Whether we are dealing with the so-called mystical experience or any other kind of experience we are bound to postulate, or take for granted, whatever is rationally implicated in the very nature of the experience on our hands.

No type of consciousness carries the implication of self-transcendence, or finite-transcendence, more coercively than does genuine mystical experience. The central aspect of it is the fusion of the self into a larger undifferentiated whole. It is thus much more the type of æsthetic experience than it is the type of knowledge-experience. In both types—the æsthetic and the mystical—consciousness is fused into union with its object, that is to say, the usual dualistic character of consciousness is transcended, though of course not wholly obliterated. A new level of consciousness is gained in which the division of self and other is minimal. But it is by no means, in either case, an empty or a negative state. The impression which so many mystics have given of negation or passivity springs, as Von Hügel declares, from an unusually large amount of actualized energy, an energy which is now penetrating and finding expression by every pore and fiber of the soul. The whole moral and spiritual creature expands and rests, yes: but this very rest is produced by action "unperceived because so fleet," "so near, so all fulfilling; or rather by a tissue of single acts, mental, emotional, volitional, so finely interwoven, so exceptionally stimulative and expressive of the soul's deepest aspirations, that these acts are not perceived as single acts, indeed that their very collective presence is apt to remain unnoticed by the soul itself."[25] Wordsworth's account passes almost unconsciously from appreciation of beauty into joyous apprehension of God and it is a wonderful self-revelation of fused consciousness which is positively affirmative.

"Sensation, soul and form

All melted into him; they swallowed up

His animal being; in them did he live,

And by them did he live; they were his life.

In such access of mind, in such high hours

Of visitation from the living God,

Thought was not; in enjoyment it expired.

No thanks he breathed, he proffered no request;

Rapt into still communion that transcends

The imperfect offices of prayer and praise,

His mind was a thanksgiving to the power

That made him; it was blessedness and love."

Tennyson has given many accounts both in prose and poetry of similar affirmation experiences, sometimes initiated from within and sometimes from without. This account from the *Memoirs* is a good specimen: "I have frequently had a kind of waking trance—this for the lack of a better word—quite up from my boyhood, when I have been all alone. This has come upon me through repeating my own name to myself silently, till all at once, as it were out of the intensity of the consciousness of individuality, individuality itself seemed to dissolve and fade away into boundless being, and this not a confused state but the clearest, the surest of the surest, utterly beyond words—where death was almost laughable impossibility—the loss of personality (if so it were) seeming no extinction, but the only true life."

Like the æsthetic experience, again, the mystical experience brings an extraordinary integration, or unifying, of the self, a flooding of the entire being with joy and an expansion which, as in the case of the highest æsthetic experiences, takes the soul out into a world which "never was on sea or land," and which, nevertheless, for the moment seems the only world.

Balfour has finely pointed out in his *Theism and Humanism*, that this expansion and joy and infinite aspect which are inherent in the æsthetic values cannot be rationally explained except on the supposition that these values are in part dependent upon a spiritual conception of the world—the experience must have a pedigree adequate to account for its greatness. We cannot begin with an experience which gives an absolutely new dimension of life and a new world of joy, and then end in our explanation with a phenomenal play of cosmic atoms—"full of sound and fury, signifying nothing."

The same thing is true with our mystical experience. We cannot, of course, say offhand that here we experience God as one experiences an object of sense, or that we have at last found an infallible and indubitable evidence of the infinite God. My only contention is that here is a form of experience which implies one of two things. Either there is far greater depth and complexity to the inmost nature of personal self-consciousness than we usually take into account, that is, we ourselves are bottomless and inwardly exhaustless in range and scope; *or* the fragmentary thing we call our self is continuous inwardly with a wider spiritual world with which we have some sort of contact-relationship and from which vitalizing energy comes in to us. It is too soon to decide between these two alternatives. We are only at the very beginning of the study of the submerged life within ourselves, and we must know vastly more about it than we now know before we can draw the boundaries of the soul or declare with certainty what comes from its own deeps and what comes from beyond its farthest margins. The studies of Bergson and still more emphatically the studies of Dr. William McDougall in *Body and Mind* show very conclusively that the consciousness of *meaning*, the higher forms of memory, the richer and more subtle emotional experiences and the more significant facts of attention, conation, and will cannot be explained in terms of cerebral activities or by any kind of mechanical causation.[26]

To arrive at any explanation of the most central activities of personal consciousness we must assume that consciousness is a reality existing in its own sphere and vastly transcending the physical mechanism which it uses. If this is a fact—and McDougall's argument is the work of one of the most careful and scientifically trained of modern psychologists—then there is no reason why what we call the "soul" might not on occasions receive incomes of life and spiritual energy from the infinite source of consciousness. I can only say that the mystic in his highest moments feels himself to be and believes himself to be in vital fellowship with Another than himself—and what is more, some power to live by does come in from somewhere. Mystical experiences in a large number of instances not only permanently integrate the self but also bring an added and heightened moral and spiritual quality and a greatly increased dynamic effect.

We are still in the stage of mystery in dealing with the causes of variations and mutations in the biological order. Something surprising and novel, something that was not there before, something incalculable and unpredictable suddenly appears and a little living creature arrives equipped with a trait which no ancestor had and by means of which he can endure better, can see farther or run faster, can survive longer, and is, in fact, on a higher life-level. We do not know how the little midget did it. But some *élan vital* may have burst in from an invisible and intangible environment, more real even than the environment we see. The universe, as Professor Shaler once said, seems to be "a realm of unending and infinitely varied originations." So, too, these flushes of splendor which break through the "Soul's east window of divine surprise" may come from a perfectly real spiritual environment without which a finite spirit could not be at all or live at all. I do not know. Our fragmentary experiences cannot enable us to furnish irrefragible proof. It only looks *as though* God were within reach and *as though* at moments we were at home with Him.

Gilbert Murray's cautious conclusion in his fine essay on *Stoicism* is a good word with which to close this chapter.

"We seem to find," he says, "not only in all religions, but in practically all philosophies, some belief that man is not quite alone in the universe, but is met in his endeavours towards the good by some external help or sympathy.... It is important to realize that the so-called belief is not really an intellectual judgment so much as a craving of the whole nature [in us].... It is only of very late years that psychologists have begun to realize the enormous dominion of those forces in man of which he is normally unconscious. We cannot escape as easily as these brave men [the Stoics] dreamed from the grip of the blind powers beneath the threshold. Indeed, as I see philosophy after philosophy falling into this unproven belief in the Friend behind phenomena, as I find that I myself cannot, except for a moment and by an effort, refrain from making the same assumption, it seems to me that perhaps here, too, we are under the spell of a very old ineradicable instinct. We are gregarious animals; our ancestors have been such for countless ages. We cannot help looking out on the world as gregarious animals do; we see it in terms of humanity and of fellowship. Students of animals under domestication have shown us how the habits of a gregarious creature, taken away from his kind, are shaped in a thousand details by reference to the lost pack which is no longer there—the pack which a dog tries to smell his way back to all the time he is out walking, the pack he calls to for help when danger threatens. It is a strange and touching thing, this eternal hunger of the gregarious animal for the herd of friends who are not there. And it may be, it may very possibly be, that, in the matter of this Friend behind phenomena, our own yearning and our own almost ineradicable instinctive conviction, since they are certainly not founded on either reason or observation, are in origin the groping of a lonely-souled gregarious animal to find its herd or its herd-leader in the great spaces between the stars.

"At any rate, it is a belief very difficult to get rid of."

FOOTNOTES

[1] Mark I. 10-11.
[2] II Corinthians III. 17.
[3] Ephesians I. 23.
[4] It is true, no doubt, that the word "mystery" in the New Testament is generally used with a technical meaning. I shall refer later to the true significance of the word, but for the moment it is not overstraining it to use it as I have done in the text.
[5] Bertrand Russell's *Philosophical Essays*, pp. 60, 61.
[6] *Ibid.*, p. 70.
[7] Arthur Balfour's *Theism and Humanism*, p. 87.
[8] *Ibid.*, p. 134.
[9] *Ibid.*, p. 273.
[10] *Ibid.*, p. 274.
[11] Tennyson's *Two Voices*.
[12] Titchener's *Beginner's Psychology*, p. 19.
[13] Dr. William McDougall's *Body and Mind*, p. 335.
[14] William James' *Principles of Psychology*, Vol. II, p. 583.
[15] James' *Psychology* (Briefer Course), p. 237.
[16] Leuba's Psychology of Religion, *p. 212.*

[17] *Ibid.*, p. 277.
[18] The World and the Individual, *Vol. I, p. 81.*
[19] *Ibid.*, p. 181.
[20] *The Aurora*, Chap. XIX, pp. 10-13.
[21] Isaac Penington, *Works*, Vol. I, p. xxxvii.
[22] Towards Democracy, *p. 190.*
[23] *Ibid.*, p. 513.
[24] Dostoievsky's *The Possessed*.
[25] The Mystical Element, *Vol. II, p. 132.*
[26] This point has been discussed in the previous chapter.

Printed in the United States of America.

CONTENTS

INTRODUCTION 3
THE INNER LIFE 7
  CHAPTER I THE INNER WAY 7
    I THE MOMENTOUS CHOICE 7
    II MAKING A LIFE 13
    III THE SPIRIT OF THE BEATITUDES 16
    IV THE WAY OF CONTAGION 22
    V THE SECOND MILE 27
  CHAPTER II THE KINGDOM WITHIN THE SOUL 33
    I BAGS THAT WAX NOT OLD 33
    II OTHERISM 37
    III SCAVENGERS AND THE KINGDOM 40
    IV "THE BEYOND IS WITHIN" 45
    V THE ATTITUDE TOWARD THE UNSEEN 48
  CHAPTER III SOME PROPHETS OF THE INNER WAY 54
    I THE PSALMIST'S WAY 54
    II THE NEW AND LIVING WAY 59

- III AN APOSTLE OF THE INNER WAY 62
- IV THE EPHESIAN GOSPEL 67

CHAPTER IV THE WAY OF EXPERIENCE 72

- I WAITING ON GOD 72
- II IN THE SPIRIT 77
- III THE POWER OF PRAYER 81
- IV THE MYSTERY OF GOODNESS 85
- V "AS ONE HAVING AUTHORITY" 89
- VI SEEING HIM WHO IS INVISIBLE 96

CHAPTER V A FUNDAMENTAL SPIRITUAL OUTLOOK 99

CHAPTER VI WHAT DOES RELIGIOUS EXPERIENCE TELL US ABOUT GOD 118

FOOTNOTES 140

P64 — To be 'saved' for St Paul is to become a new kind of person, with a new inner nature, a new dimension of life, a new joy and triumph of soul.